ISBN-10: 0692954511
ISBN-13: 978-0692954515
Library of Congress Control Number: 2017915153
LCCN Stealing History: New York, New York

I

Prologue

April 6, 1991

Twenty-five miles south of the Canadian border on beautiful Lake Champlain is Plattsburgh Air Force Base, namesake to the small state-college city in New York, adjoining it to the north. On a freezing cold night, on what would normally would have been a dark tarmac at 4:45am, was instead illuminated by several flood lights powered by the roar of nearby generators. Reporters, TV anchors and cameramen waited in mini-swarms alongside hundreds of jubilant family members.

It wasn't just another photo op for the administration, it was to be one of the biggest, the victorious heroes' welcome home from Operation Desert Storm.

The barricade was removed and there was an immediate rush by all toward the jet-lagged soldiers exiting the plane. Families embraced as news teams scoured the crowd for the most optimal faces and heart string-pulling stories for the coming day's prime-time hour.

Liz, a beautiful 25-year-old Latina brunet with fair complexion, soft features, and long jet-black pin-straight hair, screamed for Raymond as she pushed her way through the crowd to the handsome dark, 22-year-old Nuyorican solider. The two quickly leaped into each-other's arms. Like all the reunited, they kissed and embraced as if time stood still. Forehead to forehead they stood, she caressing his face with eyes closed, nervously about to ask the most important question. "So, this is it? No more military? No more traveling?"

"No. This was *it*. No more. I'm done."
Liz smiled as she nuzzled her nose to his.

"So, let's get…"
Raymond chimed in, and like any couple on the same wave-length with a promising future, together they finished, "…the fuck out of here!"

After the diminished pomp and circumstance, one can only imagine how much adulation will carry these young faces into the rest of adulthood and the changing United States workforce. For veterans, as time moves on, so will the complexity of reflection for the few who saw the brutality of infantry combat, or walked past scenes of destruction, like the infamous turkey shoot, -also known in the media as the *Highway of Death*- when U.S. planes engaged miles of retreating Iraqi military vehicles on Kuwait's route 80, as some reportedly waved white flags.

The tens of thousands who stood solely on guard for months in the Saudi desert, waiting for what was media hyped to be the bloodiest war in decades to only stroll into Kuwait and return home within 30 days, will re-examine their roles as more videos emerge of residential blocks in Baghdad reduced to rubble by smart bombs that were touted as technological civilian-saving devices.

The undisclosed number of veterans suffering from chronic fatigue and throat irritation will be a scientific discussion on whether the haphazardly managed, corporate outsourced food rations that sat for too long in the desert heat and/or the dust from exploded uranium tipped shells, would lead to the condition that would forever add *Desert Storm Syndrome* to our military lexicon, of which each theory of cause will never have an official confirmation from the government.

For years to follow, the contradiction of freeing the Kuwaiti people only to return their king to throne will be an unresolved debate between resource stability at the expense of tainting U.S. foreign policy as hypocritical, and true perpetuation of democracy, regardless of the potential worldwide economic slowdown attributed to the restructuring of an oil producing country's political processes.

As we look at these young men and women, one can only wonder how they will cope, dodge, or crumble under their realizations of history.

Raymond and Liz glowed with ear to ear smiles. Arms around each other, they stepped right into the microphone of a bleached-blond TV anchor that resembled a mannequin with the hair-style of the preceding decade.

"So, what are your plans now?" she asked with a thrust of the microphone.

The question in any other circumstance would have seemed bothersome, given the long plane ride, or overtly intrusive, considering it was the first time in months they touched, but for Raymond it was a declaration he couldn't contain, saying it clear, without hesitation and with a big smile, "Start a new life!"

CHAPTER
ONE

It was a cloudy day in downtown Manhattan. Raymond, that same optimistic solider stood glumly on a corner in a poorly fitted polyester, dark-blue bank security uniform, smoking the last of his Marlboro Ultra Lights, the type of Marlboro that tips off serious smokers to the fact that you can quit anytime but make the conscious choice not to surrender the social elixir aspect of smoking or the reason to take five from work. He held it conscientiously between his thumb and forefinger, like a joint that one burned to the end because it was the last of the stash, so as to get the last of the tobacco before the filter. Anything to extend the cigarette break of a shitty boring job. Just off to the side, a short, stout fat man in his fifties -the boss he has despised since he took the job- stepped out from the entrance of Empire Trust and Loan.

"Hey Raymond. You mind not doing that so close to the front door?"
Raymond turned expressionless to the bank manager, Mr. Hank Paulson, aka Pug-Face- Paulson, when complaining about him to the wife.

Paulson was an ugly man in face and personality, whose mustache enhanced his scowl, bringing his nastiness to the surface. That, compounded by the many or only one cheap light-gray suits and black ties he wore *everyday*, made him the caricature of a middle-management villain.

Paulson, like many in the business world and elsewhere in the workforce, felt he was destined for bigger things further up the ladder. Every year, with so many young men and women fresh out of university, holding diplomas with the ink on them still drying, willing to take a job cheap, it was clear to any man or woman in their fifties, with years out of college or with no attendance at all and making way more than those coming up, that this was pretty much the end of the line. Unlike most, Paulson would share his expectative disappointment with all, sometimes in a passive-aggressive nature, but in Raymond's case -as the only other man in the bank- *outright*.

"No problem." Raymond dropped the cigarette and extinguished it with his first step on the way to the entrance, stopping after the fourth step upon notice of the manager not moving and the accompanying extra miserable expression on his face.

The scowling man gestured with his head to the cigarette on the sidewalk. "Can you please throw that in the street?"

Raymond picked up the butt and flicked it to the street. As he attempted a second return to the front door, the bank manager turned entering, and letting the door shut in his face.

After a sigh and a pause to keep cool, he entered the bank. The clock on the wall displayed 8:30 a.m.

"Fuck," he whispered as he contemplated the length of another long, monotonous day.

.
.

The setting sun couldn't be seen from where he stood in Manhattan's Tribeca neighborhood, cornered between the skyscrapers of the financial district and its northward sprawl of only slightly smaller mega-structures that lined the West Side Highway.

What was left however was still appreciated as the hues of purple and red from the sunset lent the streets of New York a temporary look, between the white-wash glare of glass and steel of daylight and the coming mix of shadows cast between the ugly dim yellow glow of mosquito swarmed street lamps of the night.

For those who put a disciplined stop to the racing New York mind to notice, it was as if one was wearing vivid vision contacts. It could make any undented, waxed car look a little newer or transform a mediocre store display window into a work of art.

For Raymond, this vividness was a reward for a boring, mindless day's work. As a young man, it also brought out the extra beauty of many already attractive women migrating from Wall Street to Tribeca for happy hour in the growing new hip pub scene.

Raymond smiled slightly, thinking he could finally sit down for a drink with all the pretty faces he saw from the other side of the glass all day. As he pulled his keys out to lock up for the night, the bank manager hurried past without a word.

Raymond closed the door, removing the key. "Good night," he said, as he turned to see the back of the rude man walk down the block with no acknowledgment.

A handsome clean-cut man of Raymond's age, sporting a sharp black suit with perfect unmovable blond hair, approached from behind. His tie stuffed in his pocket and top collar button undone. "Hey."

Smile and relief appeared on Raymond's face upon seeing his buddy Jack McGuiness from childhood. "Wow on time."

Jack looked to the bank manager walking in the distance. "Ready for a couple of cold ones, or should I give you more time to stare at that fat fuck?"

"Been ready. Let's roll."

Raymond and Jack both grew up in Manhattan's northernmost neighborhood of Inwood. During the late 1960s through the 1970s, the neighborhood, like many at the time, underwent a shift in ethnicity. Urban flight, based on fear of crime and the obtaining of economic mobility by the predominantly Irish residents, made room for a wave of new Hispanic immigrants -mostly from the Dominican Republic- to call Inwood a home, and with time, a Hispanic community in scope with that of Spanish Harlem and the Lower East Side.

Raymond's parents, who were from Puerto Rico, spoke pleasantries with the neighbors but weren't regarded with the same inclusion as the Dominicans. What was a tolerable dynamic between parents in the community, cushioned by adult civility, was in turn brutal isolation by grade school children Speaking Spanish with strange phrases and a different accent, Raymond was called stupid by the Dominican children, was ostracized as a leper by the Irish kids and eyed as suspect by their parents every time he walked past a fruit stand west of Broadway.

Jack was the only son of progressive Irish parents. His mother was a community organizer helping those who sought integration into the community, teaching them to navigate the welfare system and signing them up to vote. His father was a representative for the Hotel and Restaurant Workers Union, of which Raymond's father and mother were both proud members.

Introduced early by their parents, Jack McGuiness was his only real friend. Raymond earned a bit of some respect on the surface from some by being an above average baseball player for both the junior and senior high school teams, but it was Jack who was there throughout, no matter what the other kids felt or said.

Raymond was never an introvert but Jack in comparison was a social butterfly, the first to strike up a conversation with strangers, the first with the guts to approach the prettiest women in the club or bar, just as he did as a kid in 83 at the roller rink across the 207th Street Bridge connecting Manhattan to the Bronx. Despite Jack relocating to Buffalo for a great sales job with the Rich Products Food Corporation, nothing had changed between them.

．
．
．

    Raymond and Jack sat at a table at the Kerry House Irish pub across from the #1, 2 and 3 subway trains, Chambers Street Subway Station. Empty bottles had accumulated before them on the small round table opposite the bar. In the midst of laughter, Raymond's face transitioned to a more somber expression. "I'm glad you stumbled into the bank last week. It's been years."
Jack put down the bottle and looked over. "Yeah, glad to be here, down state for a couple of weeks."

"Really? *Down State?* That's what we're calling the Big Apple these days?"

"Fuck this rotten apple. Yesterday I ducked around a corner to light up a cigarette cause it was windy and stepped into this cow patty that I know was homeless shit."

"Ugh! God damn." Head in hand he laughed and cough-choked on his beer. Clearing his throat, he looked up. "We got to do this every time you're in town on business."

"I promise." Jack looked from the girls at the end table to Raymond, who appeared for a moment to be lost in thought. "So...what the fuck?"

"What?"

Jack rolled his eyes and slammed his right palm to the table. "I gave you an update on my whole life. We've been people watching and goofing all night."

"Yeah, and...?"

"So, what's really going on? You seem to be putting on a game face. Like someone shot your dog and you're trying to play it off like it's not a big deal."

Raymond looked over with a smile. "Ah I'm in a funk. I had some bad business dealings. You remember Matt Conrad from high school?"

Jack quickly leaned in. "No you didn't! That scumbag?"

In embarrassment Raymond's eyes crushed shut as he sunk his head into his right hand, at the same time holding his left palm out as if to deflect further ridicule. "Yeah, yeah, I know, I know."

"So, what happened?"

"It's my fault. I had perfect credit and I let him talk me into putting up my savings to going in on a auto body place on 10th Avenue. We never had or got the right permits and the neighboring buildings weren't going to have it on the block anyway. Couldn't flip it and couldn't afford to make the notes on it, so.... long

10

story, but either way my credit is shot, wife is pissed, and I'm trying to figure out what's next."

Jack let it sink in for a moment, then turned and asked, "Is that everything?"

Raymond glanced over., his lips slightly parted, then closed.

"So, that's not everything. What happened?"

"About six weeks back, I just copped weed and...."

"Oh no."

"....some overzealous young cops shook me down as I walked home. I was only two blocks from the apartment. I even said I was a vet, hoping to get an out, but they didn't give a shit."

"And?"

"It was just enough to be more than a ticket and one more thing for Liz to be mad at. I have to appear in court next week."

"Well, it's not like you had enough on you for jail, right?"

"No, but it may be a problem with my job, should the bank ask the security firm to do a periodical background check by an independent company."

"For *that* fucken shit security job?"

Raymond took a swig. "Yeah. Go figure."

Both men sat in silence for a moment watching the crowd thin.

Jack broke the silence between them. "Not to beat a dead horse, but this bank security isn't paying your bills any better than that EMS job you had."

"At least I liked that job. I enjoyed helping people. Getting that DWI fucked that all up. And now a pot possession charge. That option is not in the near future."

"Aren't you trilingual? That's a valuable asset. Shouldn't you be a fucken loan officer there?"

11

"No one would look at me, not without at least an associate degree."

Jack, wanting to do anything to help, knew Raymond was too proud to take money or even an offer of a loan for school, grasped for any angle. "What would the military offer you if you went back?"

"Fuck that. Desert Storm was enough for me. I'll figure an easy way out."

"Hey, I just thought I'd throw it out there."

"*Sigh*....Ray, I don't know what comes easy to working stiffs. Not money, not love. But look. Even though it's been a long time, you're a bright guy that, like I said, speaks three languages. I know you, and when the opportunity is there, I know you'll seize it."

Raymond cracked a smile. "I hope so. I need a fresh start."

"You *do* need to snap out of this funk."

"I know."

"What about Liz? Last week you said she was leaving."

"Well, actually we're going to give it another try."

"Oh good. I hope so."

"Thanks for not bad mouthing her when I was telling you all about that shit going down."

"Liz is good people. And these things happen. Besides, who the fuck else would have you?"

"Ha, true."

Raymond looked to the clock on the wall. "Speaking of the wife. Hey, man, I got to run."

Jack reached out and blocked his hand as Raymond was about to pluck a couple of 20s from his wallet.

"I got this."

"Don't feel you got to...."

"I don't feel bad for your fucken ass. It's a coincidence that I'm paying. You paid last time. And you'll pay next time."

Raymond cracked a smile. "And you did drink most of it."

Jack followed with a wink as each got up from the table. "Well, that's cause you're a pussy."

Raymond dashed to the door. "Ring me and let me know when you're back in town."

"You got it," replied Jack, as he stumbled to the bar with his wallet in hand.

.

In half an hour, Raymond was jogging up the stairs of his six-story Inwood apartment building, the same one they moved into after getting out of the armed service.

Upon reaching the fourth floor and turning the corner, he came face to face with his mother-in-law, Mom-by-Mandate, as he often referred to her when complaining to Jack. Short, fat and hair as bad as the expression that she wore. She never warmed up to Raymond, but they both kept the "hi/bye" and "How are you?" civility. When she walked past him awkwardly, not making eye contact, it was then he knew. The tightening in his stomach, like a punch in the gut, was a sobering preparation for the walk through the door. From the entrance he looked into an apartment littered with packed boxes.

His father-in-law walked out of a bedroom Raymond and his wife used as an office, carrying a couple of smaller boxes.

"Hey, Paul."

The man stopped for a moment and with shame in his eyes and sympathy in his voice, said only, "I'm sorry, Ray."

Raymond liked his father-in-law. He nodded in return as they passed each-other, now walking into the more than half-empty apartment. He looked down to one of the many stacks of boxes in the living room, then up to his wife. "So much for working it out, huh?"

"Ray, I just can't do it anymore," replied Liz in a gentle tone.

Raymond pretended not to notice the petite silver heart-shaped pendent, encrusted on one side with small diamonds, *that he never purchased.* He had a feeling there was somebody else for some time, ever since losing the savings on the auto-body shop. *Or was it when he quit college? Or was it when the doctor told them that he was shooting blanks?* Evidently waring, it was obvious that adorning the pendent at this moment, was her way of saying it was definitely over for good.

He looked back down to an open box of photos. On top was a Thanksgiving holiday party and dinner from five years earlier that he and Liz had hosted. For Raymond, an only child with deceased parents, the photo quickly brought in a new depressing realization, all the extended family he had married into and how he would now be awkwardly isolated from these relationships, forcing the eventual loss of contact that comes with most divorces.

For a moment she stood still, observing the direction of his stare. Not wanting to feel worse, she didn't acknowledge it but instead continued as Raymond turned his back and walked into the kitchen, where the counter was bare of appliances, no coffee-maker, blender, not even the toaster to be found, only a small neatly stacked pile of mail.

Liz continued. "I'll be by to pick up the rest of my things while you're at work tomorrow." She then walked to the door, passing Raymond, who didn't look up as he went through what were open envelopes of overdue bills in *his* name alone.

He looked up with a furrowed brow and with an agitated tone asking, "So, you're leaving me with two months of cable, gas, electric and rent?"

"I bonded you out on a possession charge last month, Raymond," she coolly replied.

"I don't believe this shit!" With the mail in his hands and out-stretched arms, he declared, "You know I can't pay this."

"Then it's time you get your shit together. The scheming bad business ideas, losing your driver's license, the smoking weed every day, the complacency…" Now raising her voice with watering eyes. "…. all leading up to you not pulling your fucking weight in years!"

Face-to-face they stood. Liz sighed with disappointment, as she promised herself she would not get emotional.

"Please don't act like you don't understand Raymond. I know you do."
Looking down, he only nodded in return.

"My lawyer will give you a call Thursday or Friday." With a soft goodbye, she closed the door behind her.

Raymond took a long look around the apartment. Out the window, he watched as Liz got into the back of the black four-door sedan as his father-in-law loaded the last box of the day into the trunk. Once down the street, they disappeared around the corner. Raymond slowly walked into the bedroom. With the mail still in his hands, he sat on the end of the bed defeated, staring at the now empty TV stand.

He went through the mail again, approximately $3,300 in total. He called Jack but foolish pride made him hang up on the second ring. Raymond had unloaded enough on Jack tonight; asking for cash was not an option.

From the top shelf of the closet, he retrieved a notebook-size gray metal box with a four-inch depth, then reached for a small vintage candy tin, circa 1960, white, with calligraphy branding, accompanied by images of bright assorted fruit. He then returned to the end of the bed.

It had been years since he looked at the gray box's contents. For although the neighborhood wasn't that great, it wasn't that bad either.
He gazed at the weapon for a while. It was just as it was when he illegally smuggled it back to the States, pristine and probably never or hardly ever fired.

The Iraqi officer's sidearm, a Tariq pistol with Arabic inscriptions and what looked to be the head of an ancient king or general embedded as a quarter size medallion into each side of the handle, giving the imitation Beretta a very unique chicness.

He knew that with New York City rental laws he would have four or more months before the sheriff would have him put out. The immediate priority was the electric. At least he'd be able to use a microwave and toaster oven if he hit the second-hand store on Dyckman Street.

Jack always thought him a sketchy asshole but Raymond reluctantly made the call with the assumption that nothing had changed with his old baseball teammate, Alejandro, a guy who was fun in small occasional doses to smoke a joint or drink with but not trusted and kept at distance. Raymond guessed that Alejandro would still be home at his mom's project apartment, living his life as a small-time bookie. He was right.

"Ello."

"Alejandro. It's Raymond."

"Raymond who?"

"Hernandez. First base motherfucker!"

He started to laugh. "Oh snap. What up Ray? Seem you only come outta hiding twice a year."

"You know, wife and work, same old shit. How's your mom?"

"Still going strong. Always with a smile. A real old-world work horse. Women not made like that anymore."

All Raymond could think was that the poor old woman had to clean up after this asshole. "Ha. Yeah, ain't that the truth."

"She does drive me crazy with the telenovelas on all the time, yo."

Raymond had his head in his hand, not believing he had to entertain this conversation after such a shitty day. *It's her place you fucken leach.* "Yeah, that's gotta suck."

"Oh, but next week she going down to Santo Domingo to visit her sister for a week. You should come by and we could smoke up on the terrace."

Shaking his head, Raymond said, "Sounds good. Yo man. This ain't only a social call. Remember that pistol you wanted?"

On the other end, silence.

Raymond continued, "I'm cleaning house, getting rid of some stuff and I thought of you." He cringed, waiting for the pause on the other side of the line to end.

"Thought of me huh?"

17

Raymond already didn't like the tone. "Yeah, man."

"Ok I will give you five hundred for it."

"Five hundred? You offered a thousand, last time. This thing is still cherry."

"That was two years ago when you didn't wanna part wit it. I got a piece now and don't really need another."

Raymond knew he had no leverage and that Alejandro knew it too.

"So, that's it. If you want it off your hands. All three clips too."

"Ok fine. Tomorrow night I will stop by your place."

"Tomorrow? Ah….You must be jammed up." He continued through his own laughter. "I should have offered you three hundred."

Raymond, careful not to lash out, let him continue uninterrupted.

"But I will give you five if you throw in the bullets."

Wanting to jump through the phone, he said, "It takes 9mm bullets. You can get those anywhere."

"Yo Ray, I don't want to go shopping. You're not selling me an errand. I want *your* bullets."

"You want me to walk around NYC with an illegal gun *and* bullets?" Getting caught with one of the two was bad enough, with the city having some of the strictest gun laws in the country, let alone caught with both. He let the question hang out there to possibly appeal to any speck of compassion.

"Mmm, yeah, ok. You can get me the bullets next week when you come over."

"Same apartment?"

"Oh shit. Almost forgot to tell you. My grams went back to the island so me and moms took her place in Alphabet City. Bigger pad."

Raymond didn't know the neighborhood well and was only familiar with its 1970s and 80s reputation, and by the gritty 1984 movie of the same name. He had heard that some of it was now gentrified but knew Alejandro's mom would not have moved unless it was the same section 8 deal, they had uptown. It had to be the projects. Strange face in a stranger place with an illegal firearm. *Fuck that.*

"Can you swing by my job?"

"Ray, you're trying to sell me an errand again."

"*Sigh*…. How much less you want it for."

"Four hundred."

"Done. Come at 9:45. Call me and I will meet you outside."

"You lucky you my homeboy. You still at the same bank?"

"Yep."

"I always thought that with your skills and last name you would have gone pro."

"Ha. Yeah, well, shit happens. Hey, man, the wife is calling, I will see you tomorrow morn…."

"At least your ugly ass landed the hot wife of a pro ball playe…."

"Thanks man. Ok see you tomorrow."

CLICK

With the painful conversation over, Raymond breathed a sigh of relief. *What an asshole.* Raymond promised himself he was done with Alejandro as soon as he got the money. *He can buy his own fucken bullets.* He pulled the pistol from the box and held it for a moment in his shooting hand. It felt strange but there was something more, nothing good or bad but a reverence to the power it held, to open the doors for some and close them permanently for others.

He thought about the mid forty-something POW officer he seized it from. Where was he now? Was he still in the military? Career? Children? How was *his* marriage?
He now held the gun with his sleeves, wiping the prints off. He then put it in at the bottom of his work knapsack.

From the candy tin, he pulled the lighter and put the half-smoked joint to his mouth. Before today, smoking in the apartment alone would have been a small victory rather than the wound licking of defeat. Looking back to the empty stand, he needed dumb TV now more than ever, even more than the weed. He removed the joint from between his lips. Getting high in the vacuum of unhappy silence just wasn't going to do. A *Honeymooners* repeat would have been a nice treat, just what the doctor would have ordered. *Fuck!*

CHAPTER
TWO

The vibration went off halfway the jog up the subway stairs.

"Hello."

"What's up Ray? I tried calling you a few minutes ago. Everything all right?"

"Yeah, I just got off the train…"

"So, you're telling me you are late to your post?"

Raymond stopped dead in his tracks. Frustrated with his own stupidity for answering his boss, Orlando, -the owner of the security firm- before he got to the bank. He stood hand on his forehead and eyes clenched shut, searching carefully for his next words.

"Tell me you are at least close to my client."

Raymond rolled his eyes upon Orlando stressing of the last two words.

"Yes, very close to *your client.*"

"Don't be a wiseass Ray. Why did you leave a message for me to call you this morning?"

There was no more sense in tiptoeing "Can you reassign me to another post?"

"What? Ray, I just can't reassign you at this time."

"I'll go to Queens, Long Island. Didn't you land a few accounts for some stores in that mall?"

21

"I have men posted there already. I'm not just going to fuck with these mens' commute just to suit you at this time. I'm running a business and can't deal with this now. Besides, how you going to get there? Mmm? You don't drive and you're now late to a post you live *one* subway line from." Raymond walked with dead-pan expression as Orlando continued, "I don't even know what I will do with you in January because I didn't get the contract over there for next year. At this moment you have a job only because your father and me were friends."
Raymond didn't react to the pause. With the phone to his ear, he just kept walking.

"Are we done here?"
"Yeah, *sigh*.... we're done."
"Ok good. Give my love to Liz."
CLICK

On a crowded sidewalk outside the bank, Raymond puffed on the last of a cigarette, standing off to the side so as not to be seen, for he knew he was already late for work and that meant either some sort of sermon on work ethics or a snide comment was coming his way. Knowing now he was most likely to be unemployed in a few months was the icing on the morning muffin.

He felt like shit and knew he looked like shit. He wondered whether it was best that Jack hadn't picked up the phone after his wife walked out last night. For it would have meant an all-nighter in midtown with a trip to the strip club for good measure, instead of the few drinks they had already done down at the local pub. But maybe the day off with no pay would have been a fair trade.

Nearby, a middle-aged female bank teller wearing a blazer jacket with a bank pin on the lapel, finished her cigarette and walked to the door. She looked to Raymond with a smirk. "You going to wait all day or face the music?" she said, just as a school office secretary would to a child who sits a little longer on the bench before entering the principal's office for his chastisement and sentence of detention.

It wasn't fear of being fired that kept him outside the door, but rather the eroding tolerance for awkward hostility.

It was evident immediately after Raymond took the position that Hank Paulson wanted a white guard at the bank he managed. It ate at Paulson that he couldn't have fired him outright or ask that the security firm to, for fear that Raymond would go public about Paulson's ongoing affair with the senior loan officer, a threat Raymond used only because Liz wrongly believed she was pregnant three years back.

"Yes Denise." Raymond answered with snark, reluctantly following suit and stepping into the bank. Unlike the teller who hurried past, he came face-to-face with Pug-Face Paulson.

"You're late."

"I'm sorr...."

"It's not because you were shaving."

He looked Raymond up and down. "Or ironing your shirts."

The man walked away with a huff and shake of the head.

Behind the tellers, the large Roman numeral clock on the powder-blue wall read 8:40 a.m.

"Fuck, I need coffee," he whispered.

To the right, high on a wall, hung a TV tuned to the local news channel, *New York 1*, to pacify customers in line for teller service. Most of the stories were typical traffic, weather, and police blotter events that unless a serial crime or something scandalous, passed as background noise to most.

It was only Raymond who heard the details of the story.

"Yesterday evening a man was struck and killed by a bus crossing Church Street. Witnesses say Jack McGuiness, of Buffalo, stumbled out of the Kerry House bar and restaurant, intoxicated and right into traffic. Neither police officials nor the New York State Liquor Authority have said as to whether fines will be issued to the Kerry House for violation of the Alcoholic Beverage Control Law, which puts legal responsibility on a bartender and owner for cutting off customers who have had too much to drink. The New York City Department of Transportation lists this as the 147th pedestrian fatality since January 1st, putting it on track as being the worst year in recent history." The camera cut to a different anchor. *"In other news..."*

Raymond's stomach wrenched. His despair paralyzed both words and tears, giving him the appearance of having a stoic demeanor.

Outside, a distant bang could be heard as a few customers came through the door. It was barely noticed, though one old lady looked over her shoulder.

Minutes later, the typical sounds of New York Fire Department sirens became extraordinarily loud and unceasing, so much so that Raymond woke from his trance and took the stop off the door, allowing it to close. Outside the window, several firetrucks passed. Raymond stepped outside. The engines turned the corner. All appeared normal on his block but the sirens continued seemingly from all directions.

Raymond stepped back inside to see stunned customers and tellers gathered around the bank TV.

The local news reported a jet plane crashing into the 96th floor of the North Tower of the World Trade Center. Someone yelled to change the channel to CNN. The bank manager went from teller to teller, quietly asking them to get back behind the counter.

Raymond returned to the front window, observing the growing pedestrian traffic heading north as more emergency vehicles streamed south. He stepped back quickly when a second bang, this time louder, shook the glass pane and set off car alarms for blocks. A female customer watching the CNN coverage screamed, startling Raymond, who quickly turned, catching the five second delay television feed of a fireball from a plane hitting the 79th floor of the South Tower. Tellers came from behind the counter again to see the news. Many of the employees and customers were crying. Raymond walked back to the front window to observe the public's confusion outside.

He stood in what could have been perceived as a catatonic state, when the bank manager approached from behind.

"I think we should seize on this opportunity and get out of here," Paulson whispered over Raymond's shoulder, then turned to the tellers and customers. "Ladies and gentlemen, we are closing the bank. Please go home to your families."

Raymond was watching Paulson walk back to his office when he felt his cell vibrate. It was Alejandro, who, like many still in the city, may not even have known of the last half hour's events. Either way, Alejandro was not going to drive to the madness that was becoming downtown Manhattan with the five hundred, even if he wanted to, and at this point Raymond didn't care.

He went through the motions like a zombie as he locked up behind each leaving customer.
The pedestrians had crowded the sidewalk, many of whom shaken, some completely covered in what looked like white ash.
The bank manager paced alongside the counter. "Come on ladies! Let's count out and get out of here."

The sounds of sirens were deafening, even from inside the building, as many of the emergency vehicles had to creep slowly past the bank through a sea of people.
Finally, Raymond locked up behind the last leaving teller.
         "Raymond."
Raymond was unresponsive to the manager, whose eyebrows furrowed with impatience.
         "Raymond!" he called with a yell.
         "Yeah?"
         "Give me a few more minutes and we're out of here."
On the teller line TV, the news reported now of a plane hitting the Pentagon. Raymond looked back and forth between the TV and the street for a moment, then closed the vertical blinds at the door and windows. The bank manager was shuffling papers at his desk when he looked up to see the barrel of the Tariq pistol pointed at him.
         "Hands up. I want it all. No pushing buttons and no ink packets." Mentioning the ink only because he saw it in a movie.

"Raymond, what are you doing?" he asked, raising his hands slowly.

"Don't ask me stupid questions." He threw his knapsack at the man. "Fill it!"

"Ray, you're on camera."

Raymond looked to the camera, waved hello with a grin, then turned his attention back to Paulson. "Fill the fucking bag!"

"Look Ray, we all had a difficult morning. Put the gun away and I will forget…."

"Dick! You dick!" Paulson shrank back as Raymond leaned over the desk, with each word shaking the pistol at Paulson's temple. "You think I'm retarded? Fill that fucking bag!"

"I'm sorry. I'm sorry," Paulson muttered nervously as Raymond guided him by the back of his collar from around the desk to each drawer behind the teller counter.

"You got a lot of balls talking about a difficult morning. I've been here long enough to know you didn't give a fuck about any of the people working here or out there. You just wanted to leave early so your fat ass can beat everyone to the golf course."

The bank manager, unresponsive to the insult, silently finished filling the bag from the last drawer, then without a word or eye contact, held it out for Raymond.

"What the fuck? Where's the rest of it?" he asked, feeling the unexpected lightness.

"Ray, it's Tuesday and we were only open for an hour. What did you expect?"

"Don't fuck with me!" said Raymond, again raising the pistol.

"Ray," he said quietly, with palms facing up. "I swear, no bank has a lot of cash money early on a Tuesday morning."

Raymond stole a quick glance at the clock. It was a realization moment of a hasty decision that he had to rectify. "Open all the safety deposit boxes," he said, grabbing Paulson's elbow, turning the man to face the safes and following with a shove.

Paulson fumbled with the keys.
        "Hurry the fuck up!"
Raymond looked again to his vibrating phone to see it was now Orlando. He dismissed the call and texted instead. "Thank you for everything." In the next block "I'm sorry." Then powered down the phone.

Raymond started to rummage through each box that Paulson laid to a table, one by one, disappointed by what little jewelry he could find and nothing of extreme value. Finally, upon opening yet another box, to both of their surprise, it was filled with gold coins and safely packaged small gold figurines resembling gods of the Mesopotamian pagan pantheon, all of which Raymond carefully arranged with the money.
Raymond led Paulson back to his office. "Well, that's it. Get flat on the floor, facedown."
The man complied, and Raymond rummaged through a utility closet, returning with duct tape.
        "Ok fat man, time to get gift wrapped."
The bank manager postured to his knees. Welling up with tears, he pleaded, "Please Ray, don't tie me up. I don't want to be trapped here if those buildings fall. Please!"
For Raymond, it was an ugly scene that he rather not have had a part of. Paulson, once his superior, now sat before him, dejected and pathetic. The man snorted as he wept, with running mucus visible in his mustache.
        "Shut up! They were designed for this."
        "How do you know? Are you a fucking architect?" he screamed back.

"Get flat on the floor, I said!" shouted Raymond.

As the bank manager sobbed on the floor, Raymond walked over to the TV. He watched the burning buildings for a moment, contemplating the condition of the South Tower, which bellowed black smoke just above the halfway point of its height, then returned. "No. You're right. I'm not a architect. Give me your clothes and your keys."

"Please Ray. Please!"

"Shut up! I will leave your stuff at the front door," Raymond said, as Paulson started to disrobe. "Don't move for thirty minutes. Are you listening?"

"Yes. Thirty minutes."

Raymond walked to the front door, leaving Paulson face down in his boxers, tank-top and socks.

He wiped the prints from the pistol with Paulson's jacket and slid it like a hockey puck where it passed underneath office partitions into the loan officer area. He plucked fifty in cash from Paulson's wallet, dropped his keys into a garbage pail, after which he threw the man's clothes and shoes in the two different corners opposite the gun, took a deep breath, and stepped outside, re-locking the door behind him.

In the bank, Paulson, upon hearing the click of the lock, had already started to creep to the front of the bank looking for his clothes.

Outside, Raymond assessed the situation. Just to the left, downstream of pedestrian traffic, a couple of beat cops moved people along. Raymond attempted to cross the street when a ladder fire truck blocked him, forcing him to go around to the right.

Inside, the manager crawled to the front. He paused and peered through chair and table legs, looking to see if he was alone. Panning the floor for Raymond's black boots, he instead spotted his own jacket, one shoe and the pistol.

Outside, Raymond waited in line to funnel between vehicles. He let the cell phone battery and chip drop beneath the feet of the crowd and tossed the phone into the next city waste basket.

Paulson, an ex-army corporal familiar with typical firearms, raged upon finding the gun empty. "Spic bastard!"

Pulling up his pants, he peered through the vertical blinds. When the fire truck moved, Raymond was in full view, walking with the flow of pedestrians.
        "Son of a bitch," Paulson bitterly muttered.

Raymond walked at a medium pace. He turned suddenly when hearing the bank manager throw a chair through the window. He was too far from passing the police at the corner, so he turned in the opposite direction.

        "Sir, you can't walk that way," shouted one officer.
Raymond, without acknowledgment, kept walking. As he passed the bank across the street, the bank manager clumsily stepped through the broken window, knocking out another pane of glass to the sidewalk, shouting and pointing, "Hey! That man just robbed the bank!"

Raymond took off running with the two cops in pursuit. He could hear the command to stop but there was no stopping. There was a loud rumble that slowly swallowed the screams of panic. The police, still in pursuit, found it as difficult as Raymond did to move against the flow of people that had become a stampede, until coming to a corner where the crowd started to thin.

Raymond turned left and took off full stride. Suddenly, a cloud resembling a wall of debris came out from the right on the next corner, swallowing up everything in sight. The police turned the corner and upon seeing the unfolding events, ran the other way. Raymond was still in full stride, clinching his teeth as the cloud barreled toward him and him toward the cloud. Raymond yelled like a man running into battle as he entered what seemed a deadly abysmal darkness and disappeared.

CHAPTER
THREE

Primer Teniente, First Lieutenant, Roberto Montero, stood at the bow of the twenty-five-year-old Russian Stenka class, border patrol vessel, for what seemed an eternity since its early morning embarkation from an overnight porting in the sugar mill city of Puerto Padre.

The ship had long passed the luxurious European resorts of Guardalavaca on the north shore of Cuba and moved on to the less-than-humble fishing communities to the south, passing the horn of El Ramon and on to the Bahia de Cajimaya.

Montero adjusted his collar to the rise in the humidity of the inland sea. He marveled how the water still appeared clean, despite the industrialization of the west side of the bay, with its old inefficient, oil-fueled electrical generating station and the fertilizer plant just north of it.

The ship slowed, prompting Montero to reach for his large binoculars to view the bridge ahead. What national pride he was feeling turned to frustration upon seeing the little channel and wooden bridge where, as it had been mapped out, had been a much larger channel with a draw-bridge spanning the highway Cayo Saetia. From behind, a petty officer approached to inform him of the obvious.

"Lieutenant. Do you want the crew to prepare the tender to pass the channel or to go around?"
Montero looked to the sixteen-by-six-foot boat with the small outboard engine.

In a time of energy conservation and as an officer of the revolution, tasked with the responsibility to lead by example, he knows what choice he is obliged to make. *But I've paid my dues. I don't care what this kid thinks of me.*
"No. Proceed to go around," he said, turning starboard dismissively.

.
.

An hour and a half passed before the Stenka arrived at the Bahia de Lavise Navel Port. Many of the docked naval ships were still disguised as fishing trawlers, some *were* fishing trawlers, confiscated or bought by the government, each still with outriggers on either side to fool the photo technology of days long gone by, spy planes, and 1970s satellites. *The United States is well aware of this base, and we all know it, but it's better left unsaid,* thought Montero.

Montero quickly stepped from the boat, aware that all the men landside had noticed the only officer in white. He walked briskly. Young soldiers at the jetty and those about to board the ship for commissary renewal and fuel, stopped and saluted, as did others doing routine dock maintenance. Staying in stride, without making eye contact, he hastily returned the military acknowledgment in a manner somewhere between apathetic and sloppy.

Now past the hustle and bustle of the docks, he stood at the entrance to administration and officer housing. His arm was unnaturally tense holding the almost weightless black leather briefcase. Above him on an archway hung an iconic picture of Fidel Castro's head with a placard to the right reading what seemed to be a very cleverly pieced paragraph of many separate past slogans he had seen and heard over the years.-

"A revolution is not a bed of roses. The revolution is a dictatorship of the exploited against the exploiter. A revolution is a struggle between the future and the past. Each one of you must go ready to face aggression, harassment, blackmail attempts, and bribery. In the army of the workers, there must be unity; you are the officers of this army. You are the leaders."

Apart from that, was the one-word slogan that everyone who grew up on the island had seen all their lives if younger than forty and that any tourist would have seen at least once driving down any highway and if long enough, several times.

"Venceremos!" Together we will win!

From the placard he looked to the yellow administration building in the distance and to the largest cabin standing out from the white cookie-cutter ones surrounding it. To Montero, his new post looked faintly like a hotel surrounded by cabanas. It was only when he walked halfway over an eighty-by-forty-foot layout of blue tile surrounded by several seven-foot brown-tiled hexagons that he noticed what Cold War technology would have perceived as a resort pool bordered by tables with beach umbrellas.

The navel port of Lavisa is for the safe passage of all vessels entering or exiting the bay through the Boca de

Tamano. Traffic through the channel in the last five years has grown with the deepening Chinese investment in nickel mining and smelting in the heavy industrial town of Nicaro, located on a peninsula on the southern edge of the bay of Lavisa.

Northern Cuba is one of five regions in the western hemisphere to have substantial nickel deposits worthy of extraction and the only one to be in the socialist camp- the others being Ontario Canada, western Dominican Republic, northwest Columbia, and southeast Brazil.

Inside his office, Captain Diego Bartolome walked from window to window, looking out to the facility he has governed for the last two decades.
His secretary, Anabel, knocked. "Primer Teniente Montero is here."
Bartolome looked past Anabel to Montero with a smile. "Lieutenant Montero. Please come in." The two men exchanged a casual salute. "Anabel. Please don't leave. I need you to witness and document this meeting."

The secretary and Montero sat across from the captain's desk. Montero took papers from his briefcase and handed them off to Anabel, who was the first to sign and stamp regarding the date and time of receiving the documents. She then handed the papers back to Montero, who signed and initialed under the lengthy legal paragraphs regarding acceptance of authority. He handed it back to Anabel for a signature and stamp approving his signature. Anabel looked to her boss of many years with eyes welling with tears as she handed him the paperwork.

It had been a rumor for quite some time that the captain would retire. Bartolome, considered a courageous hero for his bravery and leadership in Cuba's role within Africa's theater of war, had been respected at the base and throughout the navy. It was only because of not wanting to be far from family that he never opted for a position at a more prestigious base farther up the island.

A year after the coup d'état of Angola ousting the fascist government of Portugal, the new regime in Lisbon withdrew its military from its corporate-run- already slipping away- colonies, that had for decades degenerated into economic ruin. Like many other former colonial territories throughout the world fighting for independence during the latter part of the 20th century, Angola had become a battlefield of warring organizations divided by future economic interests, armed and coaxed by the influence of the super-powers.

In November of 1975, Bartolome and Montero were young 22-year-old special forces graduates sent across the Atlantic to the capital city of Luanda in Operation Carlota. The mission was in support of MPLA, the Peoples Movement for the Liberation of Angola, against the South African Defense Forces, who along with local militias sought to keep Angola from falling into the socialist camp by advancing on the capital. It was at Quifangondo and subsequent battles that forced the surprised SADF to lose ground, allowing the MPLA to claim the following day leadership over the country. It was not however an end to the hostilities, for the two young men would continue to see the ugliness of war until a shot to the lung of Bartolome and shrapnel in the chest of Montero during the battle of Cuvelai sent them home together in 1983.

Bartolome returned the paperwork after signing and initialing in the proscribed locations. Anabel again signed and stamped as she wiped away a tear. She handed back Montero's copies.

"That will be all, Anabel," Bartolome said with a warm smile.

She got up to leave.

"Please take that across the street and upstairs," he said, gesturing to the four-story building across the walk. "And please take the rest of the day to yourself."

"But…"

"I'm not leaving until the end of the week. I'll see you tomorrow."

She returned a smile and closed the door behind her.

"Your people are going to miss you," said Montero.

"I will miss them too."

"I apologize for the delay. The map…"

"Don't apologize. I should have told you of the bridge." He leaned back and sighed. "That must have been a very old map drawn with the confidence of Soviet assistance from what seems like a lifetime ago."

"Indeed. It does seem like a lifetime ago."

Beneficial for Cuba was the disproportionate exchange of sugar -known on the world stage as the Sugar Subsidy- for the Russian Ruble and infrastructure development that sparked a boom in economic growth with the building of roads, bridges, sewer facilities, hospitals, textile factories, power plants, not to mention military expansion from the 60s well into the 80s.

Montero quickly caught himself from further talk of the deterioration of the country since the massive cut in aid from the Soviet Union after its dissolution. "Who is handling security on the other side of the channel?"

"You will be. I keep three boats in the water for oil tanker escorts to the power plant and six men at a small barrack and observation tower for a week at a time." Bartolome sensed Montero's awkwardness and tried to break the tension with his old friend. "So, congratulations on your new base and pay raise."

"And you. You're almost officially a civilian."

Bartolome leaned back in his chair with a smile. "Yes I am." He reached for two cigars from the top drawer of his desk. "Smoke?" he said with a smile, fanning the two Cohibas in his hand.

"No. Unfortunately, I must be going. That boat has maneuvers in two days. And besides, I have my wife's things to move."
Montero stood, followed by Bartolome.

"The work is worth it. I vouch for your new home's comfort. I can imagine Elicia is excited."

"Yes she is. Thank you."
Montero surrendered to the informal when he saluted but was instead met with Bartolome's hand out for a shake.

As Montero walked to the door, Bartolome sat and opened the lower right drawer.

"Oh Lieutenant," he called just as the man reached the door frame. "I think you forgot to leave me some paperwork."
Montero froze. He shut his eyes in a pause before turning. *He's not letting this go.* He turned with a nervous smile to see Bartolome pouring two glasses of Legendario Anejo Grand Reseva rum.

"Since you don't have time to smoke," he said, reclining with an ear to ear grin.
Montero sat. The two men clanked glasses and each took a more than modest sip. Montero then pulled a

manila envelope from the briefcase with a sigh. "Your contact in Spain is there now. You will go to South America after for training, then on to the Middle East from there."

Bartolome said nothing as he looked through the contents.

"How is your Arabic? Your Mediterranean post was a long time ago," Montero punctuated this with arched eyebrows.

Bartolome responded with the coolness of someone speaking with steely confidence, still not looking up from the envelope, "My Arabic, French, and English are perhaps a little rusty, but once in the surroundings, I will be fluid again. I always had a talent for language." The last sentence being completely true.

Montero leaned forward, resting his arms on the desk. "Are you sure you want to do this?"

Bartolome glanced back without a word and then again to the contents.

"Look, I know you miss your wife."

Bartolome looked up to Montero then down to the small wedding photo on his desk.

Since the fatal car crash that claimed the life of his partner of twenty-five years, not even his seven grandchildren have been able to give him comfort.

"At this time, this is what I need to do."

"Think about your pension. What if you get caught?"

"If I do not cross the interests of the revolution, I have nothing to be concerned with."

"You are a high-level military officer, leaving the country after retirement. Who will believe you?"

"You will," he said with dead pan expression.

"Yes, But…." Montero, looked down, his head shaking with clenched jaw in frustration. "Ok. What about your children and grandchildren?"

"They will be fine."

"Your mother?"

"She is with my sister in Baracoa." Bartolome smiled again, warmed by the obvious concern of his friend and his grasping at every angle to talk him out of his decision. "You've met my mother. She may out-live us both."

Both men stared at each other for a moment until Bartolome looked back to the photo.

"I need this time away from all these memories."

"But these are good memories, though. What if by doing this you end up creating bad ones?"

Bartolome peeled his eyes from the picture and looked to Montero with a smirk. "Then they'll go on the pile of ones I have from Angola."

In 1978, the Petroria government, not wanting to see the buffer zone of Namibia -a former German colony- to its northwest disappear, only to then be bordered by another anti-apartheid nation, initiated its second large offensive, Operation Reindeer.

It was the assault by the South African Air Force on the refugee camp and military outpost of Cassinga that saw the greatest number of civilian casualties via a one-day bombardment causing upwards of 600 deaths with hundreds more maimed for life, many of whom were woman and children.

Montero knew well what Bartolome referred to but made no acknowledgment of it. Their walk through the camp the following day was a painful memory that if dwelled on for more than a moment would bring back the recollection of the odor. Cutting the flashback short, he asked, "There's no talking you out of this, is there?"

"No there is not," he said, standing and walking around the desk.

Montero stood. "Well, I have to get to my boat."

The men shook, then embraced.

"Vaya con Dios, compañero," said Montero warmly.

"And you, comrade," he said, slipping a cigar into his friend's front pocket.

After Montero closed the door behind him, Bartolome sat back down, lit the other cigar and gazed reminiscently to his wedding picture as he smoked.

CHAPTER
FOUR

In a small garage, a couple hundred feet off the tropical shoreline, Raymond tinkered with a jet ski elevated on a maintenance stand, accompanied by an indigenous Peruvian man in his early twenties
Raymond let out a sigh and laid his pliers on the footboard. "All right, I'm out." Pointing at the motor, "Change these hoses on this one and lock up."

"Si, Señor."

.

Raymond unenthusiastically, entered his small pink stucco two-bedroom home, just like every day. He tossed his keys to the counter, grabbed a carton of mango juice from the refrigerator, and chugged it as he walked into the den. Upon lowering the carton from his line of sight, he stopped short, seeing a man in his lazy-boy across the room pointing a pistol at him. Raymond, with feet still, looked over his shoulder at a second gunman emerging into the entrance frame behind him.

The first gunman smirked. Then addressed Raymond in Spanish. "Hey, sit." The man stood and gestured with an outstretched arm to the lazy-boy. He continued with the condescension of arched eyebrows. "That's what you were going to do, right? It is *your* chair."

Raymond walked farther into the room to find a third gunman on his left, sitting at his dinner table. He passed the first gunman slowly, trying not to focus on the gun, but on everything in the room that could fit within his periphery of vision and took a seat in the lazy-boy, as the first gunman sat on the couch on the left, opposite the kitchen table. One gunman remained at the room entrance and other at the kitchen table. Raymond's eyes darted between the three intruders. The first gunman had the appearance of a Spanish urbanite one might find in the hip lounges of Madrid, white with long gelled hair down to his shoulders. The second and third gunmen resembled natives of mixed Indian ancestry.

"So, Raymond," said the first gunman, now in English.
Raymond looked over quickly to the reclining man.
"Oh, you're shocked?" The man then leaned forward with a wry smile. "Don't be. Sometimes the criminal world is a small one. The element you used to obtain a new identity is the same we use to find people, not to mention the trail of stolen artifacts that you were dumping along the way."

Raymond sat still and silent as he kept his eyes on the man.
"So, where's the stuff you couldn't sell?"
Raymond stared back, unresponsive.
"I'm not here to kill you, so just tell me."
"You're sitting on them," he said, gesturing with his head.

The gunman laughed, looking over to the other two. He pulled a box from under the couch, sat back down, and went through the contents, comparing them with pictures pulled from his pocket. Raymond leaned forward. Using his knees to support his elbows, he stared at the floor. The first gunman then made notations on a pad and handed the contents to the third gunman at the dinner table, who with a jeweler's optic, gave every piece a second look over. The third gunman gave a nod of approval to the first, who then looked back to Raymond.

"So, it's not like you thought it was going to turn out, is it Ray? The boat trip, paying for new identity, paying the local officials, regularly paying off the local gangsters to let you run what little business you have."

Raymond looked back to the gunman. "Yeah. I'm well aware."

"Are you also aware of the new laws passed in your country since September 11th?"

Raymond didn't answer and wasn't sure he wanted to know.

"You can never go back to the States."

That he did know.

"You didn't just rob a bank." He paused. "You exploited a national emergency at gunpoint..."

There wasn't need for emphasis on the words. It was shamefully true and leverage against him.

"...and used fake documents to cross borders. According to the new laws passed, you could be considered a terrorist, one that could have known about the plot to destroy those buildings, and took the money to give to some organization. Who knows? To a jury your stupidity would be treason."

All of it true, he thought. Raymond leaned back to one side, elbow on the arm-rest and finger on his temple. "So, what are my choices?"

"Not many. If we don't kill you, you're looking at decades behind bars. One phone call, and Interpol will be looking for you the minute we leave."

"Then…"

"Why are we still talking?"

Raymond leaned in with an expression of impatience and shrugged his shoulders.

The intruder grinned. "It's amazing how things work out sometimes," he said with a fading smile. "Under normal circumstances you never would have heard the shot." He pointed the gun as if it was just a finger.

"Our bosses are interested in your special forces training and knowledge of Arabic. If you want a fresh start, a real one in the first world, with first world identity, not this shit you bought yourself. A fresh start where you could travel freely with no worries. Move to a country with state benefits, pension, then…."

"I got the pitch. So, what are we talking about?" Raymond interrupted curtly.

"A hundred and fifty thousand for three to five months' work, and that's your cut after you pay us back a hundred. Who knows, maybe if you like, you can be full-time."

"Yeah right." The idea completely repugnant. "Where am I going?"

"All I know is that it's in the Middle East and there are more artifacts involved."

The gunman stood, pulling an envelope from his jacket and handed it to Raymond, who looked to the contents inside, a plane ticket and attachments.

"Get to the Airport in Lima. Use this ticket to a new life. Be at this address within three days."

Raymond sat staring at the ticket as the three men were leaving.

"Hey, Ray!"

Raymond got up to see only the first gunman at the front door.

"If it makes you feel any better, your business….as they say in your country, was *fucked* anyway."

"Oh yeah? Why?"

"They are going to build a couple of big hotels only three kilometers down the shore from you. Your business lease is soon to be worthless."

Raymond heard the rumors and for the most part knew it to be true. It would be worthless. His options for supporting the new life he had carved for himself were shrinking, and today he found out what he thought remained, was taken probably weeks ago at a clandestine backroom meeting, when the owner, or owners of the safety deposit box had located him.

"Am I supposed to be thankful that this time there is no choice?"

"A fresh new start Ray. A way out, that is all I'm saying."

Raymond, unresponsive, stared down to the packet in his hand, as the stranger stepped from the doorway and out of sight.

CHAPTER
FIVE

Geelong, Australia-

Charles/Chuck Emitt hung up the phone. He hesitated before turning, for he felt her eyes burning holes in his back throughout his conversation.

"So, you are going?" asked his wife, Tracy.
He turned slowly "I have to get the V-Line at noon."

"Now you go tell your son, because I won't." With that, she threw a dish towel to the sink and went outback, tending to the cloths line.

Chuck's son, Kyle, dressed in sweats and hoodie, shadow boxed into his bedroom's closet door mirror. At the age of 14 he was 5'8. His reach, along with his natural hand speed had already attracted the attention of the Australia Institute of Sports. The A.I.S. recently started a scholarship program. And although Kyle's only interest was sport competitiveness, his mother looked to the hopeful big picture of university, the only way chuck could talk his wife into allowing their son to box.

Kyle turned upon seeing his dad in the mirror. "Hey dad."

"Hey son," said Chuck, walking into the room.

Kyle, sensing his dad's change in demeanor from breakfast, asked, "Dad, you still coming to my match?"

"Not going to make this one son. I have to go to Melbourne. Last minute, about work."

Kyle nodded.

Chuck gestured to the mirror. "Ok. Hands up. Let's see your three and four combinations."

Kyle commenced punching with intermittent fades.

"Let your hands be loose for now. No sense in stiffening up your tendons during a warm up. You'll know when to close them tight." He stood behind his son in the reflection.

Kyle paused as his dad placed his hands to each shoulder. "Keep up the heel of your lead foot. Remember, your mobility is key when fighting the stocky ones. See what it does for the lead hook."

Keeping the heal elevated, Kyle popped his shoulder as his dad, with hands atop his shoulders, tuned his frame.

"How does that feel boy?"

His son smiled. "Good dad. Stronger"

Chuck gave his son a hug and a kiss to the forehead. "Good." He tussled his son's hair. "You give it hell today and you tell me all about it later at the table."

He walked out of the room with a smile. Whether Kyle made the scholarship or the Olympics, Chuck was happy his son knew how to defend himself, just as was his original intention. Anything else would be a bonus.

Chuck stepped out back, where his wife, who finished with the laundry now picked vegetables from the garden holding their 1-year-old daughter, Karen.

"I thought you be gone by now."

"I'm just going to be getting some information on a possible job."

"Don't say possible job. You know you are going to take it."

"We need the money and all this is almost over soon." He reached for the baby.

"I will believe it when I see it."

Chuck gave his daughter a kiss on the cheek. "What do you have there?" Karen raised her hand, holding up a green pepper like a found treasure. "Oh you're so good....*muah muah muah.*" She giggled with the tickling kisses to her ears. "I plan on being with the family for Christmas."

"Oh....And what of New Years?"

Chuck walked with his daughter to the house, hyper conscience of the limited quality daddy time, also knowing there was no way of selling shit to intelligent women.

.
.

Chuck walked north on Swanston Street from the railway station. He stopped and stared upon seeing the sign reading "Cat Grooming *Specialist*" He hated downtown Melbourne and its gentrification, that for the past decade crept its way to every city on Port Philip Bay. It didn't help him by appreciating the price of *his* house in Geelong's northern suburbs, but it did change the price of going out for the evening at any waterfront area.

He shook his head as he passed every hip new bar having a name that was supposed to invoke the nostalgia of -good old days gone by- working class bay town. Days he knew weren't that good. The painful memories of seeing his bloodied father and grandfather returning from the dock strikes and accompanying police clashes that led to the labor party control in 1972, cultivated his cynicism of country's economic system and that of society in general. He reached

Collins Street and into what seemed one of the last genuine watering holes in the city, the *Gateway Inn,* where he ordered Glenfiddich on the rocks and waited.

A half an hour passed before the old English man, Addy Ward, approached from behind. Getting the bartenders attention, "I'll have whatever he's having. Without the Ice." Looking to Chuck, he asked, "Do you always let people sneak up on next to you?"

"Eh. Today I don't give a fuck. Maybe tomorrow I will."

"You ruin good scotch with frozen tap water." He shook his head. "Ass." The neat scotch arrived and Addy threw down money, telling the bartender, "I got both of ours. We're gonna grab a table"
Chuck turned. "Uh oh. You only buy before you fuck me. Where am I going?"

"Every job can't have a nightlife of cheap whisky and women. Come. Let's grab the corner table." Addy laid an envelope to the table and proceeded to remove his jacket.

For a moment he just stared at the packet while Addy lit up a cigarette. Chuck was only a job away from being mortgage free and even having a seaside rental to earn some honest money for the family. The problem was, he couldn't stand it anymore. He asked, "Yemen, Saudi Arabia?"

"Close. Iraq."

"Sigh…. Who am I working for?

"Bain Thomas."
Chuck pulled out his reading glasses and reached for the envelope. "That's not so bad. Bain's alright, for a fucking Canadian."

"Bollocks. He's a fucken Yank. Tries to pass himself off as a New Brunswick Scott with that name. Can't imagine who he's fooling with that accent.

Anyway, he's been there a while now, setting everything up with a couple of guys."

"Couple of guys eh? Who?"

"You would know them as a Mr. Tino and Mr. Andre."

"Ah shit."

"Well you could have been Bain's main guy but you insisted on taking time off to be a family guy." Afraid the world spins without you boy."

"I had a kid."

"Yes. You had another, at your ripe old age."

"I'm 47 and the wife's still a looker. Jealous, you leathery geezer?"

"Nice coke bottles you're wearing. Can you still make clean shots?"

"I'm not the sniper I was but I can still point and shoot. Can still choke out anyone in this restaurant including you in your prime."

Addy, looking out the open window, blew out smoke through a grin, he then turned to the former Special Forces soldier. "You would have been far better off if you took that last job."

"Going to Honduras to kill union leaders? Really? My dad was in a union. Come to think of it…." He looked up and continued. "…. in a union with *you* Addy."

"Yes. The same union that cut a deal in 75 with the government and blackballed us, eventually leading to this. If I'm not sentimental about camaraderie and workers struggle, neither should you be."

Chuck thoughts flashed back to his country's constitutional crisis, which led to the dismissal of the Labor Party's Prime Minister and how it broke the hearts of his parents. Even as a low paid trade apprentice, he was jobless too. Quickly he snapped back to the moment, "Regardless, I was stuck with

51

those assholes in Columbia. They looked to be having too much fun, extracting info from that FARC rebel. Sadistic animals the two of them."

Addy asked with a smirk, "Need I remind you of your Job title?"

Chuck didn't need reminding that the title of welder went away with his eyesight years ago. Still, the title of mercenary wasn't yet palatable. "There's no need."

"If it makes you feel any better, *those assholes* probably don't even like each-other. So at least you have that in common with them individually."

"Thanks." Chuck opened up a passport. "So, I'm a *Michael Anderson*." A nice Anglo-Saxon name someone picked for me."

"Better that your real one."

"On with this. Says I'm going to Djakarta, all the way to Cairo to stay for two weeks, for what I will assume is my briefing, to then double back to Baghdad. Quite the jetlag. What's the job?"

"Truck driver."

"The real job?

"I don't know what's involved."

Chuck looked up again and removed his glasses. "Did you ask?"

"Of course, I asked."

"Says numbers here. This job is paying big. How can you not know? You always know?"

"Money men up the line, they put a plug on the informational channel. Not talking to us little people. Don't know what to tell you." Addy locked eyes with Chuck. "Do you want this one or not?"

"I don't like it. But yes."

"Good." Addy pushed himself from the table and reached for his jacket "You're never really supposed to like it Charlie." He placed a few dollars to the table. "The next few are on me."

"Thanks Addy."

"Fuck off."

Chuck, now alone at the corner table, sipped his scotch as he stared at the Iraqi work visa for a moment. To himself he whispered, "I fucking really don't like this."

CHAPTER
SIX

It was a surprisingly quick taxi drive from Silvio Pettirossi International Airport to the Sheraton Asunción, in the outlying neighborhood of Ycua Sati. The hotel was located on the appropriately named *Avenida Aviadores del Chaco* -Avenue of Chaco Pilots- named for the Paraguayan military aviators who fought in the first large scale aerial combat within the America's southern hemisphere. The Chaco War pitted Paraguay against neighboring Bolivia, for control of the Chaco desert, which was correctly believed -but only recently confirmed- to be rich in energy resources.

Raymond stepped from the taxi in front of the five-star hotel. Casually dressed, with a knapsack over his shoulder, he walked through the front doors. Inside was a spacious lobby but one of generic beauty. It could have been the Sheraton Ankara or Sheraton Aspen, containing nothing indicative of a city nearly five hundred years old, rich in colonial Spain and Jesuit history, and located in the only South American country where indigenous culture survived not just in the museums, but in the campo and the city streets as well, Guarani, along with Spanish, is an official language and understood by over 70 percent of Paraguay's citizens.

Upon reaching the specified room, Raymond looked back down to the paper instructions. It was a fairly swift response to the less than enthusiastic knock. In the door stood a man as young as Raymond, early thirties, neat hair, dressed in nice slacks, wearing a collared shirt that looked as if recently unbuttoned at the top. For the man still had a loosened tie on resembling the worldwide stereo-type of a young urban professional with the inability to wind down.

"Buenas, *John*."

"Uh."

"Your name *is* John. *John Nariz*. Come in, your food is getting cold."

Quickly realizing the implication that this was be his new alias, Raymond entered as John Nariz, forever leaving his former name -with no relationship with cousins, no siblings, and deceased parents- to history. As a new man, he entered cautiously, looking around the large presidential suite, then down to the silver room service cart topped with a feast fit for royalty.

"I'm Umberto. Take a seat."

Plates and food were set already at a table. John sat and unhesitatingly dug in, joining the meal, famished from the journey. Umberto took notice of John looking around the room again as he chewed on his filet mignon.

"You expected a dump? Maybe the barrio?

"Well, not this."

"Glad you like it, because you can't leave this hotel for a few weeks."

John nodded as he inhaled food. "I expect I have a whole life to memorize. Don't I?"

"And computer skills to learn. You do know how to type, right?"

"Yes."

"Ha. Good." Umberto dug back into his plate. Chewing, he looked back to John with a serious demeanor. "Good."

:

John sat exhausted at the suite's computer desk, staring at a post-it covered laptop. Paperwork and computer discs surrounded him, along with pictures and maps of Vancouver. He reached for the coffee pot he had kept at arm's length and drank from a large mug when he heard a knock and saw the door open.

"Que paso." Umberto walked in followed by another man. Umberto handed John another computer disc and paperwork to add to the collection. "Hey! What was the name of that sandwich shop that you hung out at across from university?"

"Jimmy's."

Umberto smiled and nodded to the other man, also grinning. "Nice. Are you comfortable with the programs?"

"I'm good."

"Good. I will be by tomorrow to check up on you. Put that stuff away right now." Gesturing to Captain Diego Bartolome, he said, "This is *Harry Sellenas*."

John and Harry exchanged the usual pleasantries. Harry, appearing to be a strong man of middle age, late forties or early fifties, stood about six feet two inches with dark skin and a balding afro. His English was crisp with a Spanish accent.

"Harry is staying in the room right above you, preparing for the same assignment."

There was an awkwardness as Harry and John smiled and nodded at each other.

Umberto handed John a roll of cash and took the seat at the laptop.

"I will upload this for you and lock up. You and Harry go down to the hotel club and mix it up with the business crowd. It is important that you feel comfortable and flow in conversation. You will do this every night for the remainder of your time here."

John and Harry nodded in agreement as they made their way to the door.

With a slight smile, Umberto added, "Do not get too drunk. Get club sodas or juice in-between drinks."

With all the awkwardness now completely broken, both men laughed as they shut the door behind them.

⋮

It was late at the club. Harry and John sat drinking at a table in the corner just inside from a patio terrace. No one was sitting at the neighboring tables.

"Holy shit, Harry. I can't believe the way you got that gordita on the dance floor."

"Well, I'm a good bar room compañero."

"Wingman."

"Wingman? Like air force expression?"

"Yep."

"Oh, that's funny. Hey, what did you tell her friend you were here for?"

"Tourist."

"I thought that's what you said."

John looked down to his ruby-red mixed drink. "I know. Bad, huh?"

"Well, nobody comes here for that, especially this hotel. This is a place of conventions and business closings. Any tourists would be in the old city staying at the International Asunción or the new Granados Park Hotel."

"Well, what did you say?"

"I didn't talk to as many people as you did, but I told those ladies I work for the hotel's corporate office and I was here to check on things and the workers were not to know."

"That was pretty smooth."

"It was easy. It would have been a lot harder to be a businessman because it would have required me to talk of matters I know nothing of. But if that was the assignment, I would have been prepared in advance."

"Right. How did I do otherwise?"

"Good to the untrained eye."

"Oh well, that's great."

"You have to be Johnathan Nariz. Don't worry, there's still time to grow into it."

John, slightly assured by Harry, leaned back. "Yeah, after this I still got a couple of weeks at the NGO headquarters in Canada before I ship off."

"By the time you get to Iraq…"

"What?" John interrupted, rocking the chair forward.

Harry's smile disappeared. "What? No one told you?"

John paused for composure before answering. "Whatever, man, it's cool," he sighed while looking out past the terrace to the city lights, knowing how pathetic the words sounded.

"No! No, it's not *cool*. What kind of shit is this?"

"Relax Harry."

"No! No relaxing!" Harry retorted, standing and sending the chair beneath him backward.

A few people looked over.

"Harry, just sit."

Harry paused for a moment, sat, and took a deep breath. "Look. If at this point no one told you where you are going, what else are they keeping from you, me, or any others on this assignment?"

"You and I don't know and are not supposed to know what they tell the other people. Shit, Harry! You seem to be the one who's been around the block. Why am I telling you this shit?"

Harry gave John a once-over. "You are right. I just don't want to be around halfhearted people, especially in the shit. Halfhearted turns into poor unreliable work."

"Wow, that line of talk just gave you away. This ain't the fucken military, Harry. And even if it were, there are still halfhearted people who don't believe what they're doing or joined for the wrong reasons."

"Yes. It is true." He hesitated, then proceeded to ask, "I don't want to get personal, but please tell me you were in the military."

"*Sigh*... Yes Harry."

"Advanced military?"

"Yes Harry. Fuck man, come on."

Harry shut his eyes with an inhale and opened them on the exhale, steadily regaining his cool.

John studied him for a moment. "A little better now?" he asked with a grin.

Harry chuckled softly. "Little better." A minute passed. Again, he looked John up and down. "Do you still have your appendix?"

"Umberto asked me the same thing within fifteen minutes of meeting."

"Many of security agencies around the world will mandate that operatives receive, uh...how you call...operation?"

John knew the reason but did not want to stem Harry's flow of information by appearing as a know-it-all. He was already thinking of his next question.

"Appendectomy."

"Thank you. Yes. Appendectomy, so as not to complicate a foreign assignment with unexpected illness."

"I don't have an appendix anymore. But not for the reason you think."

"No?"

"Doctors said it could have been too much movie theater popcorn in one sitting."

Harry laughed. "We may have to keep that confidential between us"

"So, let me ask you a question." John scanned the room. "Where does Umberto figure into all this? Who does he work for?"

"I think Paraguay intelligence."

"How does that work?"

"Most if not all the NGO's and religious charities are from time to time infiltrated by different intelligence agencies or mercenaries."

"Well, yeah…hello!"

"Exactly. So we know that the people we work for have men gathering intelligence and laying groundwork for probably some time. Correct?"

"Right."

"If they stumble upon something of value to the British or the Americans, they may exchange it for Argentine or Brazilian military or energy secrets. Which in turn is exchanged here for our documents and training."

"Argentine or Brazilian secrets?"

"Hey, this is a small landlocked country that can be choked with a river blockade."

John gave pause for thought and nodded in agreement, at the same time feeling naive and foolish, embarrassed that it was his first time looking at it from a political and strategic mind-set. His time as a Special Forces solider in his early twenties had been short. It was barely longer than the war he trained hard for but barely participated in.

At 22 years old and among many disenfranchised enlisted men, John listened to the many conflicting stories that milled down through the ranks explaining the onset of Desert Storm, some the official story, others of oil interests or regional power plays and still others of outright conspiracy. Still, the outcome was something John could never wrap his head around. Disgusted, he jumped at the first chance to discharge from the service, never staying long enough to comprehend how deep the backroom deals by politicians and corporations went and the complexity at which they coexisted. He asked, "And if the host government finds out about the NGO or charity?"

"They will keep a close eye on it but not bring attention to it. It's a tool everyone uses."

"What a mess."

Harry leaned back with a smile. "It's one of the world's dirtiest little secrets. An absolute taboo."

John looked back out to the city lights. "Yeah. Who the fuck would donate?"

CHAPTER
SEVEN

"Scholes, shoots…Scores!!!" Daniel, in a delayed reaction, joined the crowd that had already jumped to its feet with the forward's goal, giving Manchester United the lead over Chelsea. He knew he's been too preoccupied trying to look natural. *Stop being such a fucking amateur. Get your shit together.* He raised a smile as he took in the information of the game he was supposed to be enjoying. In retrospect: *there's a fine line between confidence and arrogance as there is between bravery and stupidity,* he reminded himself at the same time, wondering how many times he himself had been a victim of a fluctuating mix of the four, keeping him in the Provincial IRA since his late teens.

He contemplated where he'd be if his dad didn't bleed to death in a shootout with British Military in Derry when he was two, or if his older sister didn't die when a bomb was tossed into a pub, killing those sitting at a table closest to the door in 1985. That, coupled with a transient upbringing, moving from house to house throughout his childhood well into adolescence, time and again, to live behind the peace walls that since the late sixties had transformed many of the urban centers in Northern Ireland into concrete zoos, each with its pens constructed of institutional brick, but most a combination of unsightly corrugated metal, chain-link fence and barbed wire. An environment that would harden the sweetest of children. "Treat people like caged dogs, and eventually they'll bite," his mom always said.

Neither of the other two people on the mission showed any worry. Three tables ahead of Daniel sat Caleb, a young, skinny, fair skinned, and baby-faced kid from Ardoyne, who sported a clean shave and scalp, barely twenty-three and a stark reminder of himself five years and several illegalities earlier. With his cap and leather jacket and Anglo vernacular, Caleb blended into the loyalist crowed like a veteran.

Like Daniel years before, Caleb has moved up in the organization, unwavering in accepting errands and missions despite being a new father.
Daniel isn't supposed to know the intimate details of the others with him, but because of his uncle and older brother up in the leadership, he was all too familiar with the old-timers and up-and-comers. Having two young daughters never slowed Daniel down but that didn't stop him from wanting others to spend more time with their kids, at least long enough for the children to have a solid memory of their parents. He had none of his father. Often, he thought about missing both girls' first steps when detained and beaten on and off for a year in jail. He wished he took the time off. *This kid shouldn't be here,* he said to himself.

At the bar to Daniel's left sat Gene, a veteran in his mid-forties, out of shape, black hair, with a pug nose and the red stubbled face of an alcoholic slob. Gene had been way too comfortable, working on his third pint in twenty minutes. Daniel wondered and the conclusion- it has to be arrogance *and* stupidity that would allow a man to drink and enjoy a football game in such a caviler fashion as the timer ticks down on the ten pounds of Semtex in his jacket, hanging on the hook, just under the bar at his knees.

In the forty-some-odd years of heavy fighting, most of the casualties on either side of the conflict were moderate civilians, considered by both sides to be "casualties of war" or purposefully targeted as a revenge killing for those who *were* caught in the crossfire.

After so many years of fighting, the IRA doesn't expect the loyalists to set sail for Britain, nor did the loyalists expect the unionists to move over the border to a country some may never even have been to. Both sides rationalized the tit-for-tat attacks as an ongoing necessity- if not a means to an end- then at least a way of keeping the status quo of avoiding the much-believed oppression that would take place if either completely stopped.

The problem was, despite the Omagh bombing by a splinter group that killed thirty and injured approximately two hundred, those in the Provisional IRA believe that since the Good Friday Agreement and the good-faith surrendering of some weapons, attacks on unionists -even if not under official orchestration of a well-formed group- have increased not proportionally and the scales have shifted too far and need to be evened with the weight of violence.

For two years it was talked about among the leadership, but only a month ago was the plan decided upon and set into motion.

Raven's Perch Ale House in the Skanhil section of western Belfast was not only a hangout for young loyalist instigators, who on drunken evenings would launch projectiles of stone, Molotov-cocktails, pipe-bombs or just feces from sling-shots over the thirty to forty-foot so-called "peace walls" separating the Catholic unionist and Protestant loyalist neighborhoods. It was also a hangout of one of the old Glenanne Gang, Nigel Smith and two members of the Ulster Volunteer Force, Archibald Clemons and Stanley Norwich, three British paramilitaries involved in bombings and shootings since the seventies. The pub owner, Mitchel Ward, a retired, renowned, highly decorated captain of the Royal Ulster Constabulary, which operated in collusion with the paramilitaries by providing intelligence, looking the other way when it came to violence against the unionist sympathizers or families, and torturing of the detained and even as far as providing manpower to the paramilitaries.

The plan:
Gene- to plant a bomb at the bar where the four targets sat each day.

The timer- set to detonate at 4:00 p.m., which was calculated to be three or four minutes before half-time, depending upon the number of game penalties.
People may leave a game early at the eighty-minute mark if there is no chance of a comeback, but no one leaves before the half. Anything is still possible.
Daniel and Caleb- on watch for familiar faces and the attendance of women with children.

At 3:45, roughly fifteen minutes before halftime, Daniel and Caleb are to leave Gene at the pub and bring their cars across the street from the front and rear entrances, with Daniel at the front and Caleb the rear. Each to sit idling, faking cell phone conversations while on watch for the entry of women and children. If any were to enter, they would alert Gene to remove the bomb and abort the operation.

At 3:57, three minutes before detonation- Gene fakes a cell phone call and exits the bar, leaving a newly lit cigarette in the ashtray and a barely touched pint at his stool, giving the appearance of return.

The problem:

It was 3:30, and Gene had already been recognized from a fight that broke out during an ice hockey match at the Odyssey Arena a year earlier. Gene was too drunk to even remember hitting the larger man with a bottle, let alone, faces and other details.

Terence Brown, a 5'8" tall, fit, close cropped red headed man with blotchy completion in his late twenties with a sharp beak like nose, looked to Gene between breaks with pursed lips and set jaw. Sitting next to him, Chuck Harris, 6'2" also in his late twenties, with short brown hair and softer features, except for the broken bottle wound scar just below his hair-line over his left eye. Both men sat caddy-corner left of Gene with their backs to the front of the pub.

Brown leaned into Harris's left ear to whisper, "Without staring, slowly look over to the drunk, three down the bar, on the right."

From the way Brown looked and said it, Harris knew it wasn't the usual *Look at what that idiot's doing,* that prodded him to take notice of his surroundings.

Keeping a straight face, he slowly looked over to Gene and back. "Is that who I think it is? What the fuck is he doing here?" he asked with an urgent, but hushed tone.

"Don't know, but we're gonna find out and fix his ass."

Brown walked behind Gene, greeting the three old-timer paramilitaries and over to ex-Constable Ward. With a pat on the back and a request to talk in private, Ward slowly pushed himself from the bar and both men disappeared into the kitchen as Daniel looked on.

3:43- Caleb stood to put on his coat to leave. He locked eyes with Daniel, who reclined with his hands atop of head, his left hand holding his right wrist, his right pinky finger pointing to Ward's empty bar stool. Catching on, Caleb sat back down, hiding quick glances back to the bar.

3:44- Brown and Ward returned from the kitchen. There was a pulled aside conversation between Ward and the bartender and then both men were back at their stools, unnoticed was the addition of an old police issued stun gun in Brown's back pocket.

3:45- Caleb rose, followed by Daniel, who kept space between them as they exited out the front door, passing Harris and Brown, who at that moment were making their way from around the corner of the bar heading toward Gene.

Caleb turned left to walk around back and Daniel had made a right heading down the street.

Brown and Harris quietly positioned themselves behind Gene unnoticed. Nothing is thought of their hovering, as Gene's stool was directly in front of the largest TV showing the closing minutes of the first half.

The bartender standing in front of Gene, gave a subtle nod to Brown, who dug into Gene's right side with the probes of the stun gun, sending 250,000 volts through the cotton shirt, paralyzing him and sending him crashing to the floor.

"Whoa! Somebody's had too much to drink," said the bartender with a sarcastic grin.

A man on the stool closest to Gene, who witnessed the attack, threw money to the bar and hurried out.

Brown and Harris were already laying hands to Gene when the bartender interjected for those witnessing, "Will you boys help this poor man out the back."

Harris and Brown crashed Gene's head through the kitchen bat doors.

"What the fuck is going on?" asked the young cook, who reached for a pistol at a top shelf.

"Shut up Neal and just help us get him down the stairs," said Harris, out of breath.

"Does the captain know about this?"

"Of course he does!" Harris and Brown snapped back.

Neal placed the pistol behind, in the waist of his pants. Along with Brown he grabbed an arm and with Harris at the legs, they navigated the narrow way through the kitchen to the basement stairs.

Outside Caleb turned the corner behind the pub to lock eyes with Megan Ward, the captain's young, but stout wife, at the trunk of her car, which had been pulled to the back door. Megan was renowned on either side of the peace walls for her toughness as a woman and because of her paramilitary family and upbringing involving five older brothers. At eight months pregnant, she easily lifted the milk crate of whiskey with a bag of produce on top and carried it into the back.

Keeping a steady walk and eyes ahead, Caleb called Gene. He gritted his teeth as the phone rang with no answer. Caleb quickly called Daniel next, who answered on the second ring.

"What's up?"

"Megan's fucking here."

Daniel stopped dead in his tracks. "What? You sure?"

"Yeah, I'm sure. I just passed her. I called Gene and he's not answering." Daniel did an about face, heading back to the pub as Caleb continued, "I'd go in, but she already took a good look at me."

"Already on it."

"You want me to wait around?"

"No. I got it. We'll meet up later."

With an ok, Caleb hung up. Daniel snapped shut his cell and took a left into the open door at the Raven's Perch. For a moment he paused, taking in Gene's empty stool with the freshly cleaned up bar directly in front of it, then to the jacket full of Semtex, still hanging on the hook below the bar.

"Back again?"

Daniel's eyes quickly shot up to the bartender, behind him, Megan was taking bottle inventory. "Yes. Wanna hit the head one more time."

"Straight to the back," he said curtly.

Daniel walked coolly to the back and swung the door open, stepping into a quiet bathroom. He stopped to listen, then proceeded to walk past all four empty stalls, confirming his worst fears.

In the basement Gene started to regain consciousness from his electrocution to find himself taped up, hands, legs and mouth. Harris, standing over Gene bent down to peel away some of the tape over his mouth. "You remember me, asshole?"

With his back to the damp concrete floor, Gene looked up, frightened and bewildered. "No. No. Who the fuck are you?"

Harris shook his head and looked to Brown and Neal with a cracked smile. Gene, following Harris's eyes, looked to the two other men who stood to the side with pursed lips. Gene looked back, only seeing the fist cocked back for a split second before it came down, blasting him in the mouth, splitting his top lip, and knocking out front teeth.

Harris quickly reapplied the tape. "Think hard. I'll give you a minute."

In the bathroom, Daniel flipped open his cell to call Caleb. He paused, catching his reflection in the scratched mirror, asking himself why he should put anyone else in this terrible scenario and snapped the phone shut.

On the basement floor, Gene withered in pain as Brown leaned heavy on his ankle.

Neal rolled his eyes. "Stop fucking around, and ask him what his soap dodging ass is doing on our side of the fence."

Harris pulled back the tape again, giving Gene the chance to spit out teeth as he coughed on blood and gasped for air.

"It's not so bad," Harris said with a smile. "We can't make you much uglier. So, what are you doing here?"

"I don't know what you're talking about."

Again, the tape was applied, followed by Brown's stomping on Gene's ankle, the pain arching him like a creeping caterpillar.

Daniel checked his gun and extra clips in the stall. Keeping his head down, he entered the phone booth just outside the bathroom, closing the two-piece collapsible door behind him. He made the request of the operator as he shot a quick glance to the bar.

"Police Services, Queen Street."

"I need to directly speak with Special Agent Geoffrey Hanna, regarding the murder of Officer Frank Bath."

"Who is this speaking?"

"Anonymous."

"Please hold."

The official story in the papers was that while off duty, driving home from his usual watering hole, Officer Frank Bath was shot head on by a sniper.
Blocks away from the scene, one of the shooters, Stanley Leery, was later pulled over for erratic driving and speeding. As the police approached the automobile, Leery exited his vehicle shooting. He hit nothing besides the cruiser and ran off in the opposite direction, onto oncoming police arriving at the scene. Leery, for a time, made a stand and eventually succumbed to his wounds, dying from blood loss, hunkered down behind a parked car.

"Agent Hanna speaking."

"Does it burn your ass, knowing that ballistics show that there was a second shooter perched atop that trailer down the street on the north side?"
On the other end, silence. Hanna signaled to William Evens, the agent across the office, to pick up the phone on the same line.

"Does 7.62mm ring a bell?"

"I'm not at liberty to discuss the detai…."

"But I have your attention, don't I?"
Hanna paused, unsure of how to continue. *If I could just reach through this phone…*

He took a breath and said, with his voice dropping, "You have my attention."

"There are bombs at the Castle-Court mall downtown."

The two agents locked eyes. "Shit," Hanna mouthed.

Across the office the other agent started to pace, using his cell phone while still eavesdropping on the land-line. *Where is my daughter and wife today? Shopping?*

Unlike the younger Evens, Agent Hanna was only one month from the magic number of 30 of service, allowing him to retire at the age of 54 years young.

Every day on the way to work, he crunched the numbers between the soon-to-be fixed income and the retirement cottage in the small town of Ballyronan, on the other side of the island's largest lake, Lough Neagh, far across from the city of Antrim and even farther from the chaos of Belfast. Routinely weighed were the two more years of house payments against the continued grind and deterioration of Belfast and the risks it came with for the sake of a few more dollars in the pension checks to comfortably pay for it all.

His daughters, much older than Even's, had moved out of the city years before, and the wife was home cooking. Everyone close to him was in a safe place. Hanna's mind jumped from public safety to the legacy of mishandling this phone call and the months or years of inquiry that would forcibly delay retirement, then to self-disgust for focusing on such a selfish worry.

"How many bombs?"

"Fuck you! You and the rest of the goons can figure it out. It's a Saturday afternoon and you have a lot of evacuating to do. So, I suggest you get your ass moving." With that, he hung up.

Geoffrey Hanna looked again to Evens, who paced franticly with his mobile, still trying to track down the location of his wife and daughter. Before taking action, he thought, *How much can I get now for the cottage?*

Satisfied that his lie about the bombs in the mall has created a ten or more minute delayed response by the police, Daniel peered out the phone booth door, moving his pistol from his waist to his right jacket pocket.
At the bar on the right toward the back, Smith, Clemons, Norwich, and ex-captain Ward sat watching the game with their backs turned. Behind the bar toward the front of the pub, Megan and the bartender went over well stock.

He closed his eyes for a moment, taking a deep breath. At the exhale, he briskly walked from the phone booth to the back open end of the bar, getting the bartender's attention with a smiling nod and a *come here* gesture with his left hand. As close as he was to Ward and the three goons, neither of the four men paid him any mind.
The large man approached with a scowl and furrowed brow.

"Hey, I was wondering if...." Daniel reached into his pocket, pulling out his cell phone, passing it to his other hand, and then clumsily fumbled back into his right pocket. When the bartender was within four feet, he quickly pulled the pistol out, keeping it at waist level on his right side, out of view from the men at the bar, "....you've seen this?"

The blast of blood and skull fragments out the back of the bartender's head, knocked off glasses hanging above and washed across the decorative white tin ceiling.

Keeping the pregnant woman's safety in mind and with his back to the wall, Daniel raised the pistol, shooting out away from the bar at the four seated men.

Ward, Norwich and Clemons received straight-on chest shots. Only Smith turned, taking two shots through the ribs and neck before falling.

All four men in the basement looked up. Neal reached for his pistol and took off up the stairs.

Daniel followed up, leaning over the bar, shooting Clemons, who twitched on the floor.

Even through the panic of the fleeing crowd, Daniel still heard the pump of the shotgun to his right. Megan turned and leveled the sawed-off 12-gauge, getting off a narrowly missed shot as Daniel dove over the bar and another two as he ran for the swinging kitchen doors.

Daniel crashed into the kitchen stumbling, as Neal just emerged from the stairwell, pistol tight to his chest. Daniel, still in motion, with his arm already extended and raised, got off three rounds, one hitting Neal in the chest at the top step, sending him falling back down to Brown and Harris.

Daniel ducked behind the prep table, knowing Megan was shooting behind. His watch showing 3:54.

Kneeling beside the stairway, he plucked a frying pan from beneath the prep table and flashed it into the line of fire of Brown, who positioned at the base of the stairs, fired nervously, hitting the pan out of Daniel's left hand. "Shit!" he said in reaction to the shock going through his hand.

A shot from Megan blasted a large hole through the bat doors and into the wall above his head. Megan screamed incoherently as Daniel crouched behind a fryolator.

"Where is he?" Daniel shouted down to the basement.

"Let us out of this basement you fuck, or we'll bleed him out."

Behind Brown, Harris was already on the cell phone calling for help. "No, I don't know how many there are of them."

Daniel sat back against the wall with the basement staircase to his left. He leaned forward to peer through the hanging pots of the prep table to the bat doors to the right and then settled back. In a momentary trance, he listened to the roller coaster of emotion that was Megan's lamenting for her husband, from moaning to crying to screaming and back again.

"You gonna let your friend die down here, you piece of shit?"

"Fuck you! I got the upper hand. I got the high ground. You throw your weapons up."

"Suit yourself. Ok. Cut off his dick," Brown said to Harris, loud enough for the sake of Daniel's attention.

Only seconds later, Gene cried out as if his mouth had never been taped.

Daniel winced as he sat between the stereo horror that was Gene's screams of fear and pain and Megan's wailing of despair. He contemplated surrender until additional shots to the kitchen from Megan snapped him from despondency, as buckshot scattered food, cans, and shattered dishes.

"Megan! There is a bomb at the bar. It's...." Last moment wisdom cut himself off from giving the detonation time, realizing it could be used against him.
From below, Brown listened, eyes twitching with the gravity of the situation. Behind him, Harris stood up from a pantless Gene, shaking the blood off his knife, looking over.
"Save yourself and the baby!" yelled Daniel.
Another shot blasted through the kitchen doors, hitting the fryolator.
Brown fired off two shots to the door frame to the left of Daniel. "Let us out of here, you piece of shit!"
Gene's moans quieted and slowly stopped. Additional shots from Megan cleared a shelf of plates below a heat lamp and opened wide the microwave.

Daniel opened a five-gallon bucket of vegetable oil to his right and, with his foot, pushed it to the edge of the stairway. Brown hit the bucket twice. From the bucket two spouts of oil pooled at the top step and slowly dripped down. Daniel hooked his foot around low, kicking the bucket with his heel, knocking it over. Harris joined Brown at the landing as oil now cascaded down the stairs to the basement. "Shit. How we getting out of here?"
Two more shots cut through what was left of the swinging kitchen doors.
"Megan. Think of your baby!"
"Fuck you!" she screamed manically and fired another shot.

On the road, Caleb sat at a stoplight. Across the intersection a car whipped around traffic. Inside, four men, one with a ski mask, visibly holding a machine gun. But Caleb knew they were all armed. They blew the light and passed him, heading in the direction to the Raven's Perch.

"Shit!" After the car disappeared around the bend, he did a K-turn. Driving with his knee and accelerating, Caleb loaded the magazine into the 1974 AR-18.

In the kitchen, Daniel struggled to move the fryolator around him as a shield. His watch showing 3:57

Caleb followed the white Honda Accord full of armed men at a distance of two hundred feet. They stopped short when a box truck leaving a parking space on the left cut them off. They cut the wheel to go around when a pickup truck passing in the other direction forced them to hit the brakes, leaving them at an angle. Caleb floored it, slamming the right rear quarter-panel of the Accord, spinning the car to where both driver's sides faced each other. From five feet across, Caleb emptied most of the magazine. In a flash, the inside of the Accord became a tornado of blood splatter, seat cushion and tempered glass.

With his ski mask pulled over, Daniel peered through the bottom of the prep table through the hanging skillets and utensils to the bat doors, knowing that once he attempts to move the fryolator around the door frame and down the stairs, he will be exposed to Megan. It was quiet, but he could hear her reloading.

"Hey. You in there?" Caleb called, fifteen feet from the back door in a kneeling shooter's position with his ski mask pulled over.

"Yeah. Don't shoot," Daniel yelled, turning his back to the bat doors, laying both hands on the machine and pushing it. Shots from Brown blasted holes in the fryolator, spilling more grease as it came around the door frame. Megan fired off three shots, one shot skimming the left shoulder forcing Daniel to lay flat.

"I said get out of here, you crazy bitch!" he yelled, turning and putting six bullet holes at knee level through the door. On the other side of the fryolator, Brown and Harris charged up the stairs. Daniel, with a final push, sent it over.
Both men were met with the hot oil and the heavy weight of the appliance as it tumbled the stairs, pushing them back down to the basement.

Daniel moved past the stairwell to the exit corridor. He looked back over his shoulder to the bat doors. Behind him, silence. No cursing, crying, or movement.

"Let's go!" Caleb yelled from outside.
Daniel checked his watch, 4:00
As Daniel exited the back, he dove to the left. The explosion, a small fraction of a second later, passed by on his right, blowing out fire and debris. It was as if every car alarm for blocks surrounding had went off.

.

Each time they slowed down when turning to take a main road as to avoid attracting attention was when their hearts raced the fastest. Looking back, it seemed a blur as they navigated the streets from the Skankil weaving north through Cliftonville, avoiding the peace walls and their accompanying police booths and cameras to the small unionist neighborhood between Antrim and Cavehill Roads. It was there that they pulled into an open bay at a mechanic shop. With a subtle nod to the owner, they shut the overhead doors and made the phone call.

The cars in the other two bays were removed. It was only a half hour before two older sedans pulled in, each driven by women appearing to be in their late sixties and bearing sibling resemblance.

With neither informed of destinations or how long it would be, Daniel and Caleb embraced before each settled into separate locked car trunks. After the initial anxiety of claustrophobia, Daniel tried to embrace the darkness and sleep, he was exhausted mentally and physically. Keeping him from sleep at first were the few bumps on Shore Road that hurt his shoulder until he shimmied up to his side, but the discomfort was quickly replaced by thirst and a need to urinate. The trunk finally opened behind a garage at a marina. After which, it was an evening of seasickness from the bay city of Carrickfergus to the Scottish port city of Ayr aboard a haddock fishing vessel.

:

In Ayr, above a gutter installation and repair shop, Daniel sat shirtless, gritting his teeth as the boat captain cleaned his wounds, removing the few buckshot, his only surgical instrument, an alcohol sterilized pocketknife. The owner of the fishing vessel and the local liaison argued as to how to get him to the large industrial city of Glasgow as if he wasn't there. The boat captain thought it best to drive. The liaison said he had other matters to attend to and that Daniel should be given a baseball hat to keep him out of face shot from the station cameras and take the train. Daniel knew not to put in his two cents with the old-timers and ruffle feathers.

In the end, he was given clothes, petty cash for train tickets, an address, a baseball cap, reminded like an amateur not to look up at any cameras, and sent on his way.

It was only after a gyro and a beer in the lower working-class neighborhood of Possil Park did he collapse onto a lumpy old mattress in his third-floor apartment hideout, sleeping through the remainder of the first day and all night.

.
.

The knocks to the door were in the correct sequence, but stronger this time, unlike the tap of the old lady who has brought food and toilet paper up to him for the last three weeks.

Jumping from his bed, Daniel reached for the pistol and leap atop the kitchen chair with the quietness of a cat and leaned over the refrigerator he earlier positioned in front of the door. He leveled the gun to head height.

"Daniel." a voice called from the other side. "It's Uncle James."

Daniel pulled the string attached to the doorknob. The door opened eight inches before stopping at the back of the refrigerator.

"My wife and kids?" he immediately asked nervously.

"They're well. Still in Belfast, but moved in with good people to keep an eye out."

Daniel let out a sigh as the tension released. He rested both elbows atop the refrigerator. Dropping his head, he rubbed both temples.

James Caven stared blankly for a moment, then raised a slight smirk along with a takeout bag from The Baby Grand Bar and Grill, a renowned steakhouse just inside the beltway and asked, "You going to let me in?"

Daniel looked at the takeout, then further down to the other two bags aside his uncle's leg, one from the supermarket filled with groceries and the other from the pharmacy. He returned a smile of yellow teeth upon spotting the toothbrush among other toiletries through the clear plastic.

:

Daniel pushed the fork throughout the plate, garnering what was left of the garlic mashed potatoes onto his last piece of steak. As he savored the last chew, he set down the plasticware to the paper plate.

Caven reached for the roll of paper towels. He tore a couple of sheets off, handing them to his nephew, who wiped his face. "Better?"

"Better," Daniel replied, leaning back and taking a swig from the fresh bottle of seltzer.

"Aside from the bad shepherds pie twice and cheap Chinese food once, I've had nothing, but beans with rice and cabbage for three weeks."

"Old Rose does what she can with her government subsistence until we catch up with her. Her dad was an old-timer when I came in, and he died in battle for the struggle. Many people have hidden out here over the years. She's one of us till the end."

Feeling guilty of what may be interpreted as ungrateful, Daniel nodded in a gesture meaning to express concurring respect.

In an awkward moment of silence, Caven looked to Daniel, choosing his next words carefully. "I'm sure you realize the wife is leaving you."

"I figured as much."

"She's not bad-mouthing you. The kids think you're away working, and she talks about you every day to them." Daniel looked down as his uncle continued. "She's a good woman,"

"I know," Daniel softly acknowledged, revealing a slight shake to his voice.

"She's moving south of the border, in with some relatives in Cork."

"When?"

"The Ulster government was playing games at first with the paperwork. Hoping that you may turn up for a visit, they had surveillance vehicles parked out there every day for a while. They're gone now. They have no reason to keep her there, and it looks bad to do so. So, she should get the go-ahead this week."

"You have a cell phone set up for me?"

"Of course." He pushed a phone across the table. "So, young man....you caused quite the stir downtown in an effort to save Gene and occupy the police."

Daniel smirked.

"You also left your car a block from the scene of the crime."

"I'm sorry."

"Don't be. I know you were up against the clock. Literally. You were caught either way, because the damning rest of course, is that enough people went through that phone call and compared it to the description of the shooter at the bar and your file."

"I figured."

"And of course you've changed your life forever."

"I know."

"All may not be lost yet though. There's been a discovery at the crime scene."

Daniel's eyes narrowed, cocking his head to the side, he asked, "What do you mean?"

"Directly below the bomb, in the basement, there was a thin patch of concrete and soil that was cleared by the explosion, exposing the remains of two bodies. Quite the scandal, considering forensics say the bodies have been there less time than the proprietor has owned the establishment, *coincidently,* the highly decorated ex-constable, Captain Ward" Caven paused momentarily, carefully watching his nephew as he processed the information. "Gene went out like a tough guy, I'm told."

"That he did."

"Fucking savages. Shame. Anyway, I'm trying to get it worked out where if I contain the human-rights watchdogs and participate in helping their scandal going away, you may get an under-the-table pardon. But of course, you'll always unofficially be in the cross-hairs. Especially from a -not soon to retire- and embarrassed, Agent Hanna, once he comes off administrative leave. Sources say you really fucked his pension plans." Daniel and his uncle exchanged a smirk. Caven continued, "It will, however, allow you to at least come in and out of Ireland periodically to visit your children. It's not a normal family life, but....did you ever think it would be?"

"No."

"Most people think they'll accept the situation they take a chance on creating for themselves....then when they find themselves in the muck, they don't. But you've accepted your lot?"

"I have."

"Good. Then it's on to business. I can't have a good soldier sitting around collecting dust and getting fat on bad food. If you're not able to work in the six counties, then I need you at least to bring in money for the struggle. Something has to pay for the weapons and all this luxury," he said with a grin and out-stretched arms. Caven pulled an envelope from his jacket pocket and passed it across the table.

Daniel pulled the contents and spread it out in front of him.

Caven perceived his nephew's confusion. "Some kind of archeological theft. My contact in Libya mentioned it, but was reluctant to set it up. I went around him and had a Russian associate make the arrangements. Turns out it's actually a group venture of some English super elite."

"English?"

"What do you care? You're hiding in plain sight already," he said, pointing to the window. "Never forget that the super elite have no country, no borders, their back-yard is wherever they can steal. Besides, you're going to be so far down the chain of command no one is going to know where you come from."

Daniel stared at the paperwork. "Says here I'm going to Oslo, then Moscow, then Baghdad. That's it? Baghdad? What the fuck?"

"Major infrastructure overhaul going on there. I was told the job would be wrapped up in about six months. Even after the organization takes a piece, it's still a lot of money. I even got you a job running telephone wire, the same job that you had in Belfast."

Daniel sighed. "Yeah, I guess."

"There is no guessing, Daniel. Money for guns and bribes to get you contact with your family soon, doesn't just come from just donations."

"Ok I don't guess, I'm fucking thrilled."

Caven smiled at the sarcasm. "Good. I'll leave you to your phone call." Caven pushed himself from the table and stood, followed by Daniel.

"What else did they find at the pub?"

Caven's voice flushed with agitation. "You know what they found at the pub, Daniel. Nine dead men!"

"And a woman," Daniel said, interjecting.

"*Sigh*…. Yes. A woman," he replied, softening his voice.

"Did the coroners say she was shot?"

"Shot in the leg, yes."

Daniel looked to the floor. "She was pregnant."

Caven walked around the table, placing a hand on Daniel's shoulder. "My boy. She wasn't leaving, no matter what you did. Even after she was shot, she could have crawled out the front at any time. In the irrationality of despair, she made up her mind to stay there and die, even though pregnant with child. The longer one participates in a messy struggle such as ours, the greater the chances of hurting children, or in your case, a pregnant woman."

"Has it happened to you?"

"To me, to your uncle Tommy, even your father. For most, it only happens once."

Daniel looked up to his uncle, giving a nod of understanding.

"Never forget you're a good man and good father, Daniel. Remember the truth is *we all* kill every day. Every day with the taxes we pay to a government that pushes the agenda of international corporations by way of bombs and missiles. Every day with the petrol we consume in our automobiles, propping up those same corporations, along with the puppet despots in the Middle East, each with their own secret police goon squads crushing political dissent. Most of society is unaware of the indirect role they play in the killing machine. As soldiers, we affect people directly, but the woman was an accident. Guilt is a paralyzing virus to the soul. Don't let guilt paralyze you from continuing to be a good man and father. You have no choice, but to carry on for your daughters. Tomorrow is a new beginning, if you let it be." Caven pulled Daniel in and the two embraced. At the offset, he touched the cheek of his nephew and turned for the door.

"What of Caleb?"

Caven stopped, looked first to the floor, then to Daniel. "He wasn't as patient as you. He left a safe house in the country to visit his wife and new-born. Military intelligence caught up with him and he died shooting it out. Another shame."

"Yeah."

Each was quiet for a moment.

"Make your phone call. Your wife may not have the stomach for the work you do anymore, but she understands the importance. Your children will too when they're old enough. Tell them you'll visit in a few months and give them a kiss for me." With that Uncle James turned his back, quietly shutting the door behind him.

CHAPTER
EIGHT

In a narrow alley, a box truck sat idling. In the back, John sifted through the truck's packed contents of cardboard boxes with two French delivery-men, Louis and Remy.

Louis, a clean-cut, stocky middle-aged man, with light blond balding hair, is spry compared to his slightly younger, but older looking partner, Remy.

Remy, unshaven and unkempt, a tall man with short, balding brown hair, only worked at half the speed and perspired twice as much. Both helped John finish unloading boxes off the tail-gate.

John looked down on the couple of four-foot stacks and asked, "Louis, is this it?" He knows not to ask Remy, who appears depressed the last few weeks and has just quietly been going through the motions.

"Sorry, everything else is on back order or rationed this month."

"Oh, well, I'll tell Sue at the end of the day."

"Yeah, that may be a good idea," Louis said with a laugh, as he and Remy walked back to the truck cab while John started to go over the delivery. "See you in a couple of weeks or months. Who the hell knows?" yelled Louis, as they rolled off.

"Better be sooner," John replied with a smile, but serious undertone.

The truck beeped as they exited the alley, making a right and disappearing onto the street.

John looked down to the two short unopened stacks. "Shit," he muttered in anticipation of the mood this would set with the boss. He wheeled the hand truck of supplies through the back door of the NGO clinic.

On the walk to his cubicle, which doubled as a stock area, John passed Anna, a young coworker and Iraqi native. "Is that all the...."

"Shush."

As well as Anna and the boss liked each-other and bonded, it was the frustration with conditions of state austerity and economic embargo that had her walk away, shaking her head and anticipating an office blow-out.

John wheeled the hand truck to his cubicle. He stood over his desk, looking down to all the paperwork that accumulated on it since the morning, when a bead of sweat dropped from his head to a medical voucher. He straightened up and stepped back, about to use his shirt, but instead opted to quickly and inconspicuously wipe the perspiration with his hand, knowing how bad it would have looked to his boss and the patients.

Over the partition wall, at the front of the clinic, his supervisor Sue, a beautiful Asian physician, conversed in Arabic with a mother and her two children, who were reluctant to step any farther from the clinic lobby toward the private office for immunization shots. John smiled as he watched Sue speak softly to the boy and girl of ages four and five, explaining the importance of medicine and how "Mom would never let anyone hurt them," after which Sue brought the immunization shots to them and each took the shot with a whimper, but without a tear.

Sue, who at times stressed out to the point of crankiness, was still living a dream realized. Growing up in British Columbia, being a pediatric doctor was something she spoke of as far back as elementary school. While her friends were at the ice-skating rink or the movies, Sue, as young teen, babysat on weekends, using the opportunity to study as soon as the kids were asleep. It was never parental career influence that kept her focused, as neither parent was in the medical profession. Rather Sue's schoolteacher mother, Quyen, who while never cracking a whip, thought it important to regularly reiterate something that is a hard sell to any child, the importance of study for the life one wants, even *if* school comes easy.

Sue, the first daughter of professional French and English-speaking South Vietnamese immigrants, who although politically centrist, decided upon seeing the writing on the wall, that whether a takeover or merger of the North happened or not, the region would be plagued with instability of vying powers for decades to come.

In the end it wasn't the legal connections that Sue's father, Thuan Phu Trai, had made over the years as a business lawyer in Saigon that got his family a new life across the globe, but rather, it was his tenure as a piano player at the Notre Dame Basilica in downtown Saigon. As a personal friend of the bishop, Sue and her parents were given a room at the Italian embassy before embarking for Vancouver, Canada and spared standing outside western embassies for days on lines that appeared as still as the international newspaper photos of them, before the later recalling of diplomatic staffs and closing of doors.

Although Trai was a Buddhist, the innocent second job as church piano player for a little extra money would later prove fatal for many only two years later, when those of the peasant class who were Buddhist would persecute Catholics -or in his case associated- for what was years of harassment, exclusions from higher political seats and good paying jobs, both in the public and private sectors, and unequally harsh prison sentences for those who spoke of change.

It was a twist of fate that Trai, looking only at the best option of upward economic and educational mobility without political or idealistic motivation, saved himself from possible persecution. When staying in uncomfortable quarters at the embassy for only the reason of avoiding his wife's family's discouragement toward immigrating, never did he imagine the many who would later beg to be in the same cramped quarters, some out of fear for their lives.

It was because of this twist of fate that Trai raised his children with a belief in *the luck of the draw*, to feel appreciation when chance bestowed a blessing in one's favor and empathy for those upon whom it bestowed a curse.

Trai said it first to his daughters and then occasionally later as a professor of political science at the University of Victoria,
> *"Least expected is the blown thin veil between good and bad fortune over your head, leaving you on the other side until the next coming wind...."* adding the suffix *"whenever that may be."*

To his daughters it was what seemed like a pretentious fortune cookie proverb in line with an old oriental Confucius movie stereotype. Said around friends, it made them cringe, but they knew the saying truly embodied his philosophy on chance and theirs as well.

John walked past to the front door as Sue gave out candies and made small talk with the other moms. He turned, asking in Arabic, "Anybody want tea or coffee?"
All replied no.

The new health clinic, was already a recent hit with the neighborhood. Many said hello as John made his way to the café along the busy Baghdad street.
"Ello John. Another coffee with ice?"
"Yes please."

John felt appreciated in this almost middle-class neighborhood. He often heard the conditions from social workers in the organization, who stationed in some of the poorer sections of the city -where religious conservatism prevailed- were met daily with scowls of suspicion rather than smiles.

John squinted as he walked back to the clinic in the direction of the extreme desert sun. Before stepping back inside, he looked to a digital thermometer displayed in a store window across the street reading 29 degrees Celsius. Considering the dryness, John judged it to be approximately 85 degrees Fahrenheit.

To the left, in a doorway leading to the apartment above, a man of his own age, missing a leg emerged on crutches. This wasn't the only person missing limbs he saw since arriving, but one of many men, women and children. The ages ranged between early teens to the elderly, clearly showing the time-line from the last war to present, clearly dismissing random car accidents. For a moment John stared at the man, contemplating the crapshoot that is life, the war and his responsibility as a participant as he watched the young man greet his friends or family seated on the sidewalk, making his way around a table with surprising agility.

Sue noticed his changed demeanor upon his re-entering the clinic.

"What happened?"

"Oh….it's spring in Baghdad."

Sue's over-blown expression of sympathy was pure condescension. "Hold on. Let me tell the people who live here."

She relayed the complaint to the mothers, who all laughed as John meekly walked past to his desk, as one of the mothers shouted, "You just wait for August!"

John rolled his eyes and sank back into his pile of disorganized paperwork.

.
.

That same night, Sue bent over John's shoulder as they both read through invoices. John casually pointed out the obvious.

"I can't believe this stuff is not here yet. Shit!"

The clinic was quickly running low on the essentials of sterilization fluids, insulin, penicillin, and syringes.

"Come on. Tomorrow's another day."

"Did you purposefully wait until the end of the day to show me this?"

Busted? "No."

Sue threw up her hands. "Ok, let's just go."

Walking Sue to her car had become a ritual at this point for John. It's not the first night that they had found themselves awkward and at a loss for words.

In a kind tone, Sue broke the silence, "I stopped last week, but I'll ask from time to time. Do you need a ride?"

"Nah. I got to toughen up. Remember?"

"Oh, I was joking. It was unseasonably hot toda…."

John interrupted. "Sue, I know you were joking."

Sue blushed as they both exchanged smiles.

"I like to walk, but I will take you up on it one day."

He watched Sue drive away, wondering how long he could hold off on making or accepting a pass with such a bright, beautiful woman. With a sigh and a turn on his heel, he walked off down the dark street to the place he would call home for now.

．
．

John had learned to sleep through the talking of neighbors in the hallway and out front of his five-story apartment building in an old, but still middle-class neighborhood. It was 10:00 p.m., but because of the high unemployment rate of men over fifty, many passed their time sitting outside, at folding tables and chairs, drinking coffee and playing dominos.

Children who were too young to be out after dark chased one another up and down the stairwell in mock shootouts or congregated in the hallways to play with whatever ball they could find to play a mini version of soccer at each landing, the ball regularly hitting the doors and walls. Only continuous knocking at the door startled him from bed.

With the lights off, John tip-toed to the door with kitchen knife in hand. John looked through the peep-hole at Daniel Sullivan, the skinny, clean-shaven man with brown hair in his late twenties.

"Truant Officer John. Time to get to school," he said in a thick Irish accent.

With a sigh of relief, John put down the knife and opened the door. "Come in."

Daniel stood with a smile. "To what? The fucking dungeon?"

John flipped on the lights and proceeded to get dressed. "About time you got here."

"The anticipation is killing me too mate."

The young man walked about the apartment. "I shoulda been willing to pay more for a place."

John looked over with a grin.

"My place is a shit hole." He looked out the window. "My neighborhood is a shit hole too."

John, now dressed, poured both of them juice. "So, what do I call you brogue?"

"Patrick Donnelly."

John nearly choked on his drink. "That's the name they gave you?"

"I know, pretty cliché."

"Yeah." John turned off the lights and shut the door behind them. Pausing for a moment in the dim florescence of the hallway he asked, "How about I just call you *Irish*?"

"Uh….Yeah, I can live with that."

.
.

As Irish drove, John watched the transition from congested row-home flats and apartments to a neighborhood of closely spaced, but well-manicured single-family homes. Irish cut down the middle of one block through a garbage pickup alley, stopping behind a line of three parked cars leading up to a single-story white stucco house.

As both men walked to their anticipated destination, two men, Iraqi natives, one of average size and one much larger than the other, looked on from a car opposite the house across the alley.

"We got our own indigenous thugs. Class-act operation," whispered Irish.

He and John then came through the back door, giving a nod to Andre, a tall, well-built, stone-faced man with thick dark hair in his early thirties. The door locked behind them.

At the kitchen counter stood Bain, a rough looking man with a round face and long white hair in a ponytail in his mid-fifties. Bain, gave the occasional "yeah" and "no" into what appeared to be a regular black flip phone pinned between his shoulder and right ear as he continued to go through paperwork, never looking up. "Is that everybody?"

"That's it boss," replied Andre in a Slavic accent.

"Ok everybody, introduce one another. I'll be with you shortly," announced Bain. With that he snapped shut the phone.

John and Irish walked into a spacious kitchen area.

"You thought I had a nice place?" said John.

At a table, Andre took a seat with his partner Tino, a large, dark, ferocious looking, pocked faced man with close-cropped salt and pepper hair. Joining them, an average looking man in his late forties with combed over blond hair, who sat awkwardly, until his partner, Harry, walked out of the bathroom, surprising John.

"Hey, Harry."

"Johnny. How's Baghdad treating you?"

John introduced Irish, and Harry introduced Charlie Emitt as *Mike*.

"Have you met Bain yet?" asked Mike in an Australian accent.

"Who?" asked Irish.

Mike gestured to the grumpy older man at the kitchen island. "Bain Thomas. the chief."

John leaned in. "Oh no. We figured we'll let him mix it up when he's ready."

"All right fellas. Please take a seat."

"Speak of the devil," whispered Irish.

Bain remained standing at the kitchen island as if it was a podium. The rest sat at and next to the tables. "I'm glad everybody made it to sunny Baghdad without a hitch. Some of you have heard rumors of artifacts and assumed this to be some kind of tomb-raiding mission. It's a bit more complex than that." Bain paused, then continued.

"As you know, the United States made its business to invade and occupy Afghanistan. Iraq is next. We will raid the Iraq museum of history during the bombing of Baghdad."

Bain gave a long look to the silent, but concerned faces. John squirmed in his seat. Only Tino and Andre appeared expressionless.

"I see I have everyone's attention. The U.S. will bomb Baghdad, then seize the southern oil fields up to Najaf."

Dead silence.

"Do you trust this intelligence?" questioned Mike.

"The bosses would not invest in this if they didn't know it would happen."

"That's not what I asked."

"I know what you...."

John interrupted. "I think the question is why now and how can they?"

Bain continued, "Saddam has been a bad example of U.S. foreign affairs. With all the odds stacked against him, he's managed to keep this sand-box afloat using state sponsored land reform for farming and nationalizing other sectors of the economy. America doesn't want another embarrassing Fidel Castro type in this part of the world. Saddam is also going to start taking the Euro for oil, making investors on Wall Street and generals in Washington very nervous. If things remain on track, it is estimated there will be a large loss of U.S. influence throughout the region."

"When is this supposed to happen?" asked Andre.

"Two months."

"Two months?" John replied in quick reaction. "How are they going to get Congress behind it?"

"Through a false-flag incident in Israel or Jordan that will be blamed on Al-Qaeda operating in Iraq with government complicity." In frustration, Bain let out a sigh. "Hey, fellas, you guys have all been around the block. Big oil wants it, big oil gets it. The U.S. and Britain are already in Afghanistan. They seize Iraq and put the economic squeeze on Iran without ever having to face a real army. It's going to happen."

"Do you have an exact date?" asked Tino in an Arabic accent.

"Narrowed down to the last week of May."

"How will we know?" asked Irish.

"I'm told we will definitely know when it happens. That's when we rally together and wait for reprisals."

The men stepped on one another's questions.

"What are we talking about?" asked John.

"You don't need to know that now."

"How are we getting out of here?" asked Mike.

"By ambulance to a pumping station outside Najaf. We wait for a private U.S. security force to take us by chopper to Dubai, where we get the rest of our cash and go our own ways."

"What about check-points?" asked Harry.

"When the job goes down, the assault will be quick. Saddam won't have time to set up check-points, let alone get dug in to fight. Most soldiers will be scrambling to get home to their families. The few stragglers that are left we'll blast out of the way."

John looked down, trying to hide his disgust.

"I want you to realize this is no more dangerous than robbing a bank during the day."

Irish smirked. "So, how come the local gangsters don't do it?"

"Good question," whispered John.

"First, they couldn't get the items out of here. Second, the crime families here are on our payroll. They think we're here to rob a bank and are expecting a cut on top of what they already get for strong-arming. And that's the third thing, no guns until show-time."

Eyes glanced at one another, obviously uncomfortable with the arrangements.

Bain continued, steamrolling over their dissatisfied murmuring, "You guys don't want to get caught with guns here. Anyway, this meeting is about getting you paired up and doling out assignments. Only three of you speak Arabic, so it's Tino and Andre, John and Patrick, Harry and Mike." Bain started handing out envelopes to the men. "In here is your spending money and a number to the off-shore account. Make sure the first deposit is in there tomorrow."

Harry peeked in and grinned to John. Bain handed John his packet. "You're only getting spending money this time around. They said you know why."

98

Andre looked over with a wiseass smile. "You must have really fucked up."

Aside from a roll of the eyes, John didn't acknowledge the crack as he kept his head down, going through the contents.

Bain started handing out cell phones to each of the men. "The numbers on the back. I want you guys to hang out with your partner. Get to know each other. It could save your lives. After your bullshit jobs, scope out the locations listed, weekends too. Four eyes are better than two, but I don't want more than two of you in the same place at the same time. This is important."

All the men nodded in agreement.

Bain continued. "Ok. Case the museum in and out, the streets around it, the parking lots and garages. That's it fellas. In a month we'll meet again to go over our findings. Be careful."

Bain turned his back and the men rose to leave. He looked over his shoulder, addressing only Tino and Andre, "You guys stick around."

In the alley Mike, Harry, Irish and John walked to their cars.

Harry gave a big smile and a friendly pat on John's arm with the envelope. "So, the adventure begins," he said, walking past to Mike's car, with a shrug of the shoulders and shaking his head with a snort.

.
.

Later, Irish pulled up to the corner of John's block.

Irish was the first to break the silence. "You haven't said a word."

"I got a lot to digest."

"Do you think…."

John quickly and curtly cut him off. "I don't know. But we just got paid. So I think we should just go through the motions." He closed his eyes and took a deep breath, leaning back against the head-rest.

Irish understood and looked on in silence, letting his new partner regain composure.

Halfway out of the door, John looked over his shoulder, "I guess you'll pick me up tomorrow?"

"Yep."

Irish sped off as John walked down the quiet, dark street in contemplation of the mess he had gotten himself into.

CHAPTER
NINE

The following day, John reclined with a drag of a cigarette on a bench in a semi-enclosed bus stop, relieved he was able to break out early with Sue at a meeting at the General Hospital. Afternoon rush hour had not started yet, and John enjoyed the quiet until it was shattered. He turned quickly to the screeching of a near accident and blowing horn. John shook his head, seeing Irish beating the steering wheel, then throwing up his hands and yelling at other motorists.

Irish pulled up, and John stepped on the cigarette and jumped in. "So, much for low profile."

"Yeah, yeah, yeah."

"The museum?"

"Yep."

John watched Irish guzzle coffee as he recklessly sped through congested streets. "How much of this Arabic coffee you been drinking?"

Irish avoided another near-miss accident trying to beat the yellow light as they crossed an intersection, with a dip, putting the car briefly airborne and down hard. He looked over. "Too fucking much."

At the same time Harry and Mike looked for a parking spot by the museum.

Harry perked up. "Let's scope the streets around it first."

After a couple of blocks, Mike made a right turn. "Ooh, look at this." he said, as they passed a mobile military post, which was no more than a military dressed 20x9 foot temporary office trailer with hitch that one may see on a large construction site. "I'm sure there will be a lot more soon."

"Let's remember where it is and write it down." Harry reached into the glove box for his pen and pad.

"Why? The post has wheels. It can move ten times before the job. Don't write anything down. What if we get pulled over and searched?"

"I thought of that already. Maybe we can see a pattern," he said, jotting down the location in illegible Spanish.

Harry looked to Mike, expecting a response, but none came. Mike drove around the other adjacent blocks of the museum. Each saw nothing else of interest, circled back around again close and parked.

As the men began their three-block walk to the museum, the briefing and Harry's recent assessment weighed heavily on Mike, who struggled for a moment on how to phrase the next question.

"So, Harry, we're going to hope these people are creatures of habit?" Mike asked with the condescension of a parent or teacher.

"People *are* creatures of habit."

"Putting up checkpoints *isn't* supposed to be in a pattern."

After a pause, Harry, not wanting to argue, said, "Let's hope Bain is right. Caught by surprise, most will abandon their posts."

"I don't like jobs that depend too much on hope," Mike replied seriously, looking straight ahead as he led the climb up the museum stairs with Harry following.

Harry felt compelled to break the silence and the awkwardness of now looking to Mike's back. "Without further intelligence, everything is a gamble. All we have is hope or the choice to go home."

Mike didn't reply.

Inside the museum, Irish and John stood awestruck at the immense collection. Throughout the corridors, clusters of students from throughout the world, accompanied by professors, listened to lectures on the many exhibits.

Irish looked over. Nudging John, "Hey, to your left."

John peeled his eyes from a beautiful statue to see Harry and Mike about fifty feet away. John made eye contact with Harry, who gave a slight nod of acknowledgment and turned to Mike.

"Already overlapping?" said Irish as both men watched Harry and Mike walk in the direction of the front entrance.

"Yeah, that will happen sometimes."

John and Irish looked back to the art when Sue walked up from behind and taped John on the shoulder.

"Hey," said John, with wide eyes.

"I thought you were going home."

John stammered at a loss for words, forcing Irish to interject, "He doesn't mean to be rude. I'm Patrick, but please call me Irish."

"Yeah. Nice going, Mr. Manners," said Sue, backslapping John in the chest. "Pleased to meet you. I'm Sue."

"Have you been here awhile?" John asked, with regained composure.

"Yeah. I'm taking off though. I just got a call from corporate. Well, you boys soak up that culture," she punctuated with a wide grin.

Irish returned a nod and smile and again the two men were back on the job.

"Very nice. Your coworker?"

"My boss." John, still taken aback by the encounter, rolled his eyes. "Let's do a couple of laps around."

"Seems friendly."

"We appear non-threatening."

"Why do you say that?"

"Because I've been dodging flirtation since the second week working with her."

"And?"

"And now I'm caught in a museum with you on the sneak."

"Oh, so what?"

"Why would a single grunt turn down an awesome hot doctor? She thinks we're gay, stupid."

CHAPTER
TEN

It's another hour before sunset, when John and Irish walked out from a multi-story parking garage. Irish, a few paces ahead of John, stopped and turned, giving the structure another glance. "So, what do you think?"

John walked past Irish without a second look. "Last one was better."

"We've been at this a couple of weeks now. What's wrong with this one?"

"See the building on the corner? It's a mosque. This block isn't quiet enough for a vehicle switch. How many more on the list?"

"Half dozen."

"Shit man. Day's over. It'll be dark in an hour." John opened the car door. "Cruise me home."

"I think we got time for one more," said Irish at the wheel. John rolled his eyes.

As Irish drove, John turned, then paused, unsure of how to phrase the question without seeming more naive or inexperienced than he was or appeared already. "Why didn't we get satellite phones instead of cells?"

"Huh?"

"We are going to count on cell service in this country, with all its dead zones? These guys are already funding a ton of cash into this job. What's the cost of satellite technology for seven men?"

"Well, we're not going off into the wilderness. And service seems to be good for all of us in the city, so.... As for the cost, no it's not a lot of money, considering. But it's not a perfected technology. In some cases you need a direct line of sight to the satellite. If you're indoors or on a narrow street with three stories of buildings on both sides, you have little access to the sky. Lastly, it's illegal."

"Ha! Like the gun stipulation."

"Worse than the gun stipulation. Which I'm not happy about, but understand. Imagine we were pulled over now. Two foreigners, mind you, English speaking foreigners, with satellite phones? With guns, we're thrown in jail for twenty years. With satellite phones, we're treated as potential spies, tortured and in solitary confinement for who knows how long and eventually shot."

"Bain should at least have one."

"He may. Or the person he reports to may. Some countries, they will let you get a permit, but this operation doesn't want to give the security services anything to poke their nose into. And it could be that setting up a satellite phone here may attract the attention of the big-boy security agencies like MI6, the CIA, or whatever the fuck the Russians call their spooks now."

John let the information sink in for a moment, then said, "Well, we are going off to Najaf. That's pretty much the wilderness between here and there."

Irish smiled, "The goal is not to be separated during our trek" Irish turned to John, his smile fading "or the possible preceding gunfight we may have pulling this whole thing off." Facing forward, he continued, "I know there are holes in the theory of how this is

106

supposed to go down. But believe me...." John pretended not to notice Irish swallow a lump in his throat. "....there are holes in the theories of every plan like this." Smiling again, "The idea is not to fall into those holes."

As they approached a traffic circle, Irish noticed the car ahead was Tino and Andre's. "Ha! Look at this. More familiar faces."
John knew this was his way of signing off from the serious conversation. Irish, like a teenager, rode their tail and whipped around them, honking. Both men shot dirty looks as they exited the circle in the other direction.
      "Wow! Two fucking sour-pusses, huh? You're lucky to be paired up with me," he declared with absolute conviction.
John just looked over as Irish, still speeding, approached a construction zone that brought the road from three lanes to two.
As he began the merge, a white pickup cut them off. "Hey, asshole!" Irish yelled, as he merged, then sped to catch up with the pickup.
      "Hey. Don't fuck with these people," warned John.
Irish pulled alongside the pickup. Inside the truck, two Asian men looked over, laughing.
      "They're foreigners," exclaimed Irish. The pickup accelerated and passed them. Irish followed suit.
      "Will you please let this go?" pleaded John.
Irish caught up to the right side of the pickup and rolled down the window.
      "What's your problem, asshole?"
The man in the passenger seat brandished a pistol. Irish and John ducked as Irish blindly slammed on the breaks, veering the car to the right, hitting construction

barricades before coming to a stop on the side of the road.

"You ok?"

"Who the fuck were those guys?" asked Irish, frazzled.

"I don't know" John replied, more composed. "Construction workers?"

"With guns?"

"I don't know. Look. They could have shot us. They didn't. There's a lot of strange people from all over in this town."

"And if you're wrong?" Irish flipped open his phone "We gotta tell Bain."

"Tell him what? We nearly wrecked the car and let some guys get away. Bain ain't gonna like us calling him every time we get spooked."

Irish looked out the window, took a deep breath and snapped shut the phone. "Fuck. I hate this place."

Behind a white Citroen police cruiser rolled up behind, keeping a distance of twenty feet. The reflection in the mirrors of the police lights sat both men up straight.

"This isn't good."

"No it's not," replied John, in a whisper, as two police officers walked up on either side of their vehicle with their hands on their holstered pistols. "Just keep your hands on the dash and don't move until they ask."

"Work visas, drivers license and registration," asked the police officer in Arabic on Irish's side.

"What did he sa...."

"Work visas, drivers license and registration."

Both men fumbled in their pockets for the necessary documents.

"Look in the glove box for the registration."

John, in Arabic, made known to the police officers his intention of opening the glove box for the rest of the requested paperwork for the sake of easing tension, but neither man's hand came away from their holster.

"I don't see it," said John, as he went through its contents.

"Shit. The registrations at the apartment in that packet we got from the Ministry of Transportation."
Before John could relay the issue, the police gave the command for each to exit the car slowly, after which John relayed the commands in English for both to place their hands atop the automobile, leaning forward with spread legs to be searched and handcuffed.
Irish looked to John, who stood leaning against the car on the opposite side.
"John, I'm having one of those *should've gone to college* moments."
John looked over. His left eye twitched, but made no reply.

⋮

Separately, John and Irish gave identical statements to one of the arresting policemen and the processing officer, regarding the destruction of city property while driving on the shoulder, with the excuse of the occupants in an adjacent vehicle brandishing a weapon. When asked as to how they knew each-other and what was their business in the vicinity, each gave the same rehearsed statement for the scenario at hand- that they met a month ago when Irish came into the clinic where John worked and they were just out looking for a place to eat dinner.

The interrogating officers acted as though they were playing poker, offering not an expression or sound, just an escort back to the detainee holding area where Irish and John were re-handcuffed to a railing that ran the length of the bench that bordered the windowless, dimly lit, fifteen by forty-foot gray concrete room.

Detained with them, seven other men ranging in age from twenty to sixty awaited processing. Two of the oldest men were luckily passed out drunk or high. All else who were sober and awake had to sit silently, listening to the cries of a man getting beaten in the next room.

John sat as far forward as he could with his right hand cuffed to the railing behind and resting his head in his left.

Irish, leaning back, looked to his partner. "John," he whispered. "I'm sorry."

"You *are* fucking sorry. I told you not to chase that guy," replied John, staring straight.

"You're right."

A minute passed before Irish again spoke. "Have you ever been down this road before?"

"Interrogated and beat by cops? Yeah. As a kid. You know. Fucking up. But not this bad. What about you?"

"Yes. A few times. *This bad.*"

John looked over with no reply.

The door opened and a guard stepped in with a clipboard. "Donnally! Nariz!"

"Here we go," said John under his breath.

"You are clear to leave," said the guard in English.

Behind him, two guards dragged in the same Asian man who had run them off the road to the railing next to Irish, where they hung him handcuffed by his right hand, his feet spread out on the floor and head hanging over the bench. His blood-stained, tattered clothes smelled of urine and sweat.

Irish stared at the beaten man as the two men were un-cuffed. *"And this is why Bain warned about getting caught with guns here."*

110

"You may pick up your vehicle when you return with the registration and money for fine. If you don't pay in a week, vehicle become police property," said the guard in his best English.

"Thank you," said John. He then looked to Irish, who sat still, fixated on the man whose eyes were swollen shut to mere slits, his foot set unnaturally askew as if they had stomped his ankle broke. "Come on."

Outside the police station, Harry and Mike sat waiting under an awning.

"There they are!" exclaimed Mike, as the men exited the building. "Iraq's most wanted!"

"How did you guys know?" asked John.

"You didn't see us wave and beep as you were getting cuffed?" asked Harry with a smile.

"No."

"Well, we did."

"Does Bain know?" asked John.

"No. We took care of it," said Mike.

"So, these guys got greased? I still have a fine, and now I owe you too?"

"Yep," he said with a nod and smile.

"Whatever. I'm just glad they didn't punch me in the stomach," said Irish.

"Why is that?" all asked.

"Cause I got to take a shit," he said, laughing.

Mike cracked up and threw his arm around Irish as they walked. "Ok. Let's get this lad a toilet and then a stiff drink."

Harry and John walked, hanging back ten feet.

John gestured to Irish. "You see what the fuck I'm dealing with here? He must have been drinking last night"

"If you want to trade for Mr. Negativity, be my guest," replied Harry, with a smirk and gesture of his head to Mike.

CHAPTER
ELEVEN

Late at night and the team of six huddled around the island in Bain's kitchen as he made notations on a city road map. "If you made these choices based on observations of these locations and observations from them, then that's it. We'll use this route in, this one out, and this garage for the switch. Any second thoughts?" Bain paused and looked up to the men, all of them silent. "Ok. The trucks are parked here and here. And I will re-park them every day until the last week."

"Any idea of commencement?" asked Mike.

"Yes. The twenty-first through the twenty-fifth. I want you all to do a drive-by to get a good look at the trucks. Keep vigilant about not being followed. Do the route every day. Make sure the manholes are covered. Look for new potholes, road construction and suspicious characters."

All the men nodded in acknowledgment.

"Ok now let me show you guys the target item. You probably overlooked it at the museum. It's the first exhibit in the east wing."

Bain presented a photo of a frame holding three small stone tablets.

"That's it?" asked Irish.

Bain smirked. "Oh, you of the cultured class are not impressed?"

Everyone laughed.

"Seems that some people in Europe have figured out what these tablets say before anyone else has. Must be a hell of a story."

All grinned except Harry. John took notice.

Bain finished. "That's it. The slightest suspicious shit, call a meeting. If not, see you at show-time."

CHAPTER
TWELVE

May 23, 2002

It was midday, only a couple of hours away from peak temperature. Sweat beaded down John's face as he tried to fix the clinic's one air conditioner. Anna approached from behind, stopping short as the box wrench slipped from John's hand. "Shit!"

"Do you know what you're doing?"

"It's simple. I just have to replace this belt."

"Well, it will have to wait. The delivery guy needs help."

"Shit. I'll never get this thing fixed. Does he really need my help?"

"He is by himself today and the alley is blocked, so he has to carry the shipment pretty far. Plus, it's a lot of the stuff that we had on back order."

"Shit."

⁞

A half an hour into unpacking the box truck, John leaned on a four-foot stack.

"Are we getting close?"

"Halfway there. I gotta take a break." Louis jumped from the back of the truck, sweat soaked.

"No argument here."

At that moment, Sue walked up with a pitcher of iced tea and plastic cups.

"You read our minds," said John, with a big smile.

"Oh, I just want to keep you both productive," she replied with a grin.

"And alive," said Louis, raising his cup.

"Yes, you owe me," she said, walking back to the clinic looking over her shoulder with a wry smile.

Louis smiled. He followed Sue with his eyes as she climbed the concrete loading dock stairs. "She's a pip, eh?"

"Yep."

"Firm, but nice."

"That's her all right," said John as he sat pensively. *Please don't ask me if I'm fucking my boss yet. Please don't ask me if I'm fucking my boss yet.*

John and Louis sat on the truck tailgate, quickly consuming the pitcher.

Louis let out a sigh. "The truth is I'm more worn out than thirsty."

"I didn't want to say it, but you *look* worn out."

"Yeah, I got personal stress."

"Your partner?"

"God damn Remy. Probably in an alley with a needle in his arm. No, but he adds to it."

"Don't ask?"

"Nah," Louis looked down to his cup for a moment.

"Well, Remy does fit the look lately. Sorry."

"Yes. Me too. Not everyone copes well with being away from home and everything or everyone they love, no matter how much the money."

"Of all drugs. Seems so extreme."

116

"Well, those who do it say that the first high is like none else, so they forever chase that euphoria. Or so it is said. I don't know and never want to know."

John shook his head. "Such a throwback drug. Didn't people learn from the sixties? Can't believe people do that shit now."

"It's all about accessibility. Sometimes it's cheaper than the Moroccan hash. Ever since the Taliban were pushed out of power, heroin has been rolling out of Afghanistan and into every city from here to northern Europe. United States and Canada will feel the effects soon enough from this mess."

John had lost all anxiety regarding questions of his work relationship. His thoughts were now darting between the relationship of wars and money.

"Hey John, how did you get stuck in this dusty place? Lose a bet?"

John snapped to and smiled, thinking of an evasive, but funny half honest answer. "I was blackmailed."

"Yeah, one must be to end up here," replied Louis with a chuckle.

.

That night John woke to the sound of knocking and Irish's frantic voice on the other side. "John. You in there? John!"

John stumbled out of bed. "I'm coming. I'm coming." John opened the door. Irish rushed in waving a newspaper. "Was this supposed to be it?"

"What?"

"It! It! The false flag."

John's eyes were just beginning to focus on the print. "I was unloading a truck all day. Where am I supposed to be looking?"

"Turn it around. Front page." Irish flipped the paper around for John, who read aloud.

"A failed terrorist attack at the Pi Glilot gas facility just north of Tel Aviv could have killed tens of thousands. What the fuck?"
Irish grabbed back the paper and threw it to the kitchen counter. "Get your shit together; we're going for a ride."

.

The crew stood scattered about Bain's kitchen, Andre and Irish at the island counter, Mike against the wall, John sat with Harry on his right with Tino one over.
Bain walked in from another room. "I've been on the phone and all day chasing info. And the answer to all of your questions is yes. That was supposed to be it."
The crew grumbled. Mike, the only one to speak out, asked, "What now?"

"I'm getting to that now," replied Bain in a calm tone. "Turns out the truck driver slash detonator lived. The Israelis can't get nothing out of him because he was a know-nothing pawn, so they'll blame Hamas. If it went down like it was supposed to, it would have been so big, the U.S. would have blamed Iraqi missile fire. Just give me a second." Bain started to flip through paperwork.

John leaned to Harry and whispered, "That could have killed a lot of people." Harry nodded in agreement. Hearing the whisper, Tino glared at John, to which John unflinchingly mirrored. Harry caught on.

Bain continued. "Ok. Regarding your contract and what will happen…."

Harry leaned into Tino's line of sight and gestured with a slight nod of the head toward Bain. "Maybe you should pay attention?" he whispered in Arabic. Tino flushed red, then looked back to Bain.

"In two days there will be a deposit into your account, and your payment upon completion will be double." Andre was the only one smiling. "We're looking at…."

"Wait. Wait," interrupted Mike. "Could we not make that on a job that we know will happen?"

"It's going to happen. You just have to sit tight."

Mike sat down and Irish leaned against the wall.

Bain continued. "We're looking at September through December. There are other operations planned, but as you can see, nothing is certain. The only stable plan is that…."

"I'm gone," said Mike as he stood.

"….the Pentagon will start to feed the press stories of Iraqi complicity in terrorism as a backup. But that can take a little longer," Bain continued and showed no acknowledgment of the door slamming shut behind Mike as he handed out envelopes. "Your monthly spending money has been increased, so enjoy yourselves. Don't get too flashy. You're going to be here awhile. Don't get too comfortable with the people. I have a number to a good pimp if you need it. That's it fellas. Go home and get some rest."

Tino shot a look to Harry and John as he left the table.

"Good night," Harry said with a condescending smile and effeminate flutter of his fingers.

John looked to Irish, counting his money with the grin of a kid, then to Harry, who with a look expressed his shared frustrations.

Andre walked over toward Bain. "I'll take that number."

.
.

Later, with a third of a bottle of whiskey in him and only a couple of hours to daybreak, Mike sloppily packed a suit-case at the same time venting to Harry. "Fuck this. I can't believe I agreed to this shit. It stank from the beginning. Everything was hush-hush. Shame on me. I knew better."

Harry sat listening quietly.

"This isn't going to happen. It's a waste of time. You know I've worked with Bain before. He must be slipping and those English investors must have lost their minds. There's no invasion. Bush is stupid, but not that stupid."

"How will they just let you walk away?" asked Harry.

"If they kill me, they can't use me again. They can't get the money back. If they have me arrested, I'll spill the beans. So, fuck-em."

"I wish you luck man."

Mike zipped shut the suit-case. "You could leave too. But because you haven't been around long enough, your reputation would be ruined."

Harry made no reaction to the suggestion. "Tell me what you know about Bain and his men."

"What? Tino and Andre? Stay away. They're Bain's goons."

"No love lost, eh?" replied Harry with a smirk.

"No. None. Steer clear as much as possible and tell them nothing of your personal life."

"Tell me of *their* personal life. Their history, what makes them tick."

Mike paused and cracked a smile, thinking how much he wanted to divulge. The term *"honor among thieves"* really meant something to Mike. As far as he was concerned, mercenaries working together had to have a code of ethics, if only to each other for survival, no matter how sleazy the job at the time.

To Mike these men were not friends, but not co-workers either. They were teammates. It felt wrong to talk of their personal lives. But he liked Harry and saw the danger. It was with that reasoning Mike let out a sigh and proceeded to open the informational floodgates. "Andre and Tino both work as heavy equipment operators on the same construction site. They both got their vices, but plagued by demons of different nature. But at the same time, they're demons of a similar past. As you know, like many of the same background, drugs and antisocial behavior become the only pastime for most in this line of work."

"Of course."

"Tino was raised on the streets of Sana, Yemen. Killing for money is something he probably can't even remember not doing. He started as a teenage mercenary during the country's turbulent political and economic transition, as at that time there was a new communist regime. Probably was fighting for one of those Saudi funded groups." Getting off track, he went on, "You know old King Fasil didn't want those socialists on *his* border."

Harry stifled a laugh. "I can imagine. Go on," he said, prompting Mike to get back to the subject matter.

"The violent adolescence was typical. Compounded with the regions sexually repressive culture. For that savage, social ability never stood a

121

chance to take root. He spends his free time chasing hash or regular weed -if that's the only thing available- and throwing a beating for every purchase that seems the slightest bit light. He's a mean fucker." Mike paused to take a swig.

"Andre?" Harry asked, prodding Mike to continue.

"Andre's violent career would start later for him than Tino's. He was part of the ethnic minorities in the old Yugoslavia during that country's civil war or....disintegration if you have it. Many of the disenfranchised, marginalized, and unemployed youth were convinced to join arms with militias fighting for what the most thought to be a better homeland. *Sigh*....Well, we know what happened. Instead, it was about resource and mineral rights for wealthy backers within the new boundaries that were to make up Serbia and the surrounding new nations once Yugoslavia, *mind you*, coincidentally....the last communist government in Europe was broken up. Andre, of course, was some of the few, just in it for a piece of the pie. Promised everything and given nothing, mercenary work seemed the only option to him and for that matter, many of the other fresh seasoned fighters. For Andre's greed, the expense free life-style and good pay leaves a lot of room for his daily diet of sexual, alcohol and drug indulgence. Unlike Tino, -who mostly does hash, and drinks only when he can't find any- Andrea will eat, smoke or snort anything he can get his hands on. Somehow he still keeps it together."

"Wonderful. And Bain?"

"Ha! A busy boy Bain is. Regardless of weather or day of the week, days and nights may be spent picking up money from European liaisons and dropping off cash to the local gangsters to keep operations running. But Bain, unlike the rest, is unencumbered by a real full-time job. For this

122

assignment he has a cover of being employed as a chief of facility maintenance at a large hotel owned by....get this...."

But Harry already figured out the answer and finished Mike's sentence. "The same investors."

Mike smiled, nodding his head and continued, "That have provided his suburban accommodations *and* who have bought up the surrounding houses *and* are bankrolling the *whole* heist."

"Big bucks."

"Very big bucks. But that doesn't mean shit!" Mike's smile disappeared with a pause. Continuing, his demeanor hardened. "It doesn't mean things are going to work out right. *Especially* in this powder-keg shit corner of the world. But if I were you, I'd get the fuck out."

Harry looked up for a moment.

"I really think this is going to drag out and get ugly."

Harry sat staring off into space as Mike finished.

"A fucking disaster. But if not, I wish you luck."

CHAPTER
THIRTEEN

"What do you mean we can leave?" asked Irish as he turned around from the refrigerator with two beers, handing one off to John.

"Harry said he seemed pretty comfortable with the idea. Mike believes that his services are worth not killing him in the event that these investors need experienced men in the future, and he has enough on them to go to the authorities before they would look at him cross-eyed."

Irish put down the bottle after a long guzzle, "What do you believe?"

"I don't know. Harry says it's plausible because it takes a lot to get on the inside of a operation like this."

"Without getting too personal, did it take a lot for us to get here?" asked Irish, brows arched with a smirk.

John shrugged. "We had the credentials and recommendations."

"I'm beginning to think nobody fucking wanted it."

"Ha. Yeah, maybe."

"So, what is Harry going to do?"

"Says he's gonna stay for the money. That he can't go back now. Said his wife died. I didn't press the issue."

"Sad. Surprised he told you as much. And you Johnny boy? Guessing by what Andre said about your first payment, you owe money."

"They're paid off already. I....uh...." John swallowed the lump in his throat "....have nothing to go back to."

"Nothing? Family? Friends?"

"Dead and dead."

"Sorry to hear that."

John averted his eyes. "Clinic is rewarding and keeps me going. Fuck it. I'm staying." Shrugging and looking back to Irish, he asked, "You?"

"I got a lot to go back to. Soon, but not soon enough." Irish paused and took a deep breath. "I'm on a mission to lay low and make money." He raised his bottle, prompting John to raise his. Leaning across the table to clink bottles "To killing time."

Clink

"To killing time."

"Oh...." Irish smiled, "....and you doing me a favor." followed by a wink and nod.

:

Just after twelve noon, and John checked his cell phone for signal for what seemed to be the thousandth time since driving north from Baghdad 150 miles. Irish was right, but John assumed it was still part assumption that there would be cell service along the Tigris River for the agricultural communities that ran alongside it -though it was a much bigger assumption that there would be service on Highway 1, ten miles west of the river.

It was just east of the junction to Erbil, on Al-Quyarah Makhmoor Road, where John found a suitable pay-phone and called Irish from his cell as he approached the booth with a bucket of coins. There were no calling cards to Ireland to be found and if there were, it was assumed that some of the cards' one-eight-hundred numbers went through security services data-bases, depending upon the country called.

"I've been waiting. Where you been?"

"I was behind trucks all throughout construction zones. Don't give me shit."

"Aww you're a good man Johnny." The favor was greatly appreciated, for Irish was well aware how much he would have stood out in the rural landscape to a passing highway police cruiser.

"Yeah, yeah, yeah."

"Ok, remember what I told you."

"Already started," John said, as he loosened the transmitter faceplate mouthpiece. He stretched the transmitter cup along the handset of the phone until it was the same distance from receiver to transmitter as his own cell phone and taped the two together, receiver to transmitter of the other phone on both ends. "Testing, testing. You still hear me?"

"Yeah, I hear you."

"Ok, sit tight. I'm dialing for the operator now."

The initial call to the local operator was for free, as was the transfer of the call to the international switchboard operator, who, judging by the long pause, the repeat of the request and the hold time of ten minutes, had never before patched a call through to Cork, the island's third largest city. It was at this point a third of the coin bucket was deposited before John could hear the ringing of the phone thousands of miles away, where Daniel's brother-in-law and longtime friend, Brendan Conner, also a member of the organization, accepted

126

the unidentified call on a special designated cell phone. "Hello."

"You fat fuck, it's me." Saying the next in Gaelic, "Don't use names or ask questions I can't answer."

"Of course. Hey mate it's good to hear your voice."

"Yours as well. Listen, I'm paying by the second on this one, so, you got to quickly put me through."

"Ok."

John, keeping his chest to the shell surrounding the pay phone, peered out to what was mostly still barren landscape, aside from the occasional tractor trailer.

In Cork, Brendan dialed the number on his regular cell phone, on which he raised the volume and held it to the designated phone, transmitter to speaker of each.

"Hello."

"Shannon."

"Oh my God," she said under her breath. Startled, she placed her hand over her heart as if it had skipped a beat. She looked over to the two young girls of four and five playing in the living room. She walked out of sight and quietly asked, "Are you alright?"

"As good as a man who has been away from everyone he loves for months can be."

"It's the life you chose." Shannon braced for the possible response of- *You knew who I was before we were married!* or any variation of a *for better or for worse* guilt trip. But it never came.

"It is. And I respect and understand your decision."

Shannon swallowed the lump in her throat and fought back the tears, moved by Daniel's understanding, which at the same time was also a confirmation by him of never leaving the IRA or remaining her husband.

"Ok." With a paper towel, she wiped away the tears and cleared her throat, not wanting the girls to see or her brother -acting as the second middleman on the call -to hear the sadness in her voice. "I'll get the girls."

"Deposit please…."

"Hey, buddy," Irish nervously called out over the voice of the operator.

John was just dozing off, looking at the beginning of a desert sun-scape, when he heard Irish call out. "Ok. I'm on it," he said, rapidly putting in the coins with the rigged phones between his shoulder and head.

"Thank you."

"Daddy! Daddy!" the two girls sat ear to ear with the phone between them.

Brandon didn't listen in, but instead watched a soccer game with the sound off, occasionally leaning over to check if there was still conversation.

John tried his best not to eavesdrop, but had to listen closer for the sake of the request of a coin deposit. To John, the girls sounded cute with their Irish brogues. He thought how things may have been different if he had kids. Would he have tried harder to get ahead, held a better job and not ended up here?

On the highway, four trucks towing anti-aircraft guns streamed south in a convoy.

"Deposit please…."

John entered into the phone the remaining coins.

"Thank you."

"Hey, buddy, that's the last of the money."

"Who's that, Daddy?"

"Oh, just a friend. Ok ladies, I miss you both and can't wait to see you and kiss you both. Muah! Put Mommy back on for me."

"Hey."

"Hey." Irish paused a moment. It was strange sadness to have a conversation with Shannon as the mother of his kids and not a wife. In the hectic uprooting of his family's life since the bombing of Raven's Perch, he doubted she had the time, energy or the head to have someone in her life. The social conditions were just not there. But by her voice, he knew she was done with him and this was the tone of the future between them. "I have to be quick. We're out of coins. What else is going on? Everything being taken care of?"

"Well, it was crazy for a while with the move. We're settled in here now."

"Money? Paperwork? Kids getting along in the new neighborhood?"

"Money hasn't been a problem. The girls and I are still waiting on paperwork for progressive resident status with eventual citizenship and also for them to start school."

"What do you mean *start* school? What have they been doing?"

"Staying home with me. And the neighbors are starting to ask questions."

"What about private school?"

"We're not getting that kind of money, and I still don't have a job. What money I do get I hold on to, because you never know when someone is going to be locked up and the envelopes stop coming."

"Shannon. School isn't the business to be frugal. If you have it, spend it."

"I told you, don't have it."

"*Sigh….* Ok. Don't be too proud to make phone calls. Now is not the time to be too proud."

"I know. I will."

"Deposit please…."

"Ok, that's my cue."

"Ok."

"Deposit please…."

"Keep kissing the girls for me."

"I will kiss them for you always."

"Deposit please...."
"Thanks love."
"Please be carefu...."
CLICK
   *"Sigh....*Shit."

John knew the conversation was over and said nothing as he untaped his phone from the pay phone receiver and put its transmitter back in place. He waited for his friend to get his head together.

 "John!"
 "I'm here buddy."
 "What are you still doing there? Bring it the fuck back home. I think we both earned a drink."

CHAPTER
FOURTEEN

Evening-

John and Sue were wrapping up the day's paperwork. Both looked up when Irish pulled up out front.

"Your *friend* is here," Sue said with a coy smile.

"Yes, my friend is here. Not my *friend*," he said with the gesture of quotations.

"Then ask me out."

An-tic-i-pa-tion:
Positive or negative emotion coinciding in faith with fruition of a foretold event.

Anticipation- how one deals with it is a matter of temperament and previous conditioning, or lack thereof.

Irish- A telephone lineman by day. His and John's partnership has developed into a friendship. Doing the opposite of what Bain had spoken of, both engaged the locals with social intimacy not befitting the predicted scenario -*theft of art in the midst of chaos*. With their age as a factor -both only hovering on either side of thirty- neither is thinking of the consequences, as many nights are spent playing dominoes for small pots at the local coffeehouse.

John, going a step further, allowed his romance with Sue to deepen. She is always there to cheer John and Irish during their night league soccer at the local lit field. With John and Irish's newly raised supplemental income, all three regularly go out for dinner. The three now very close.

Harry- An ex-high-ranking military officer, pushing fifty and painfully aware of the social ramifications of the job and that a well-oiled propaganda machine has the power to bring it to fruition, lays low. When not driving a forklift at the river docks, his free days are spent at the city library and nights with history and archeological books taken out. His only indulgence is the black-market cigars he reclines with when reading.

August-
Although the story spent weeks in the local newspapers afterward, it's no wonder that Tino, who numbed out to events that would startle most, didn't raise an eyebrow when reading of the arrest of terror suspects by Jordanian authorities.

September 8th
Unlike his partner, Andre sensed the tension in the air when he walked up to a newsstand where six men were engaged in passionate discussion. As Andre reached for the *New York Times*, the men took notice of the Caucasian man and stopped talking.
He stared at the main article: *"Iraqi purchase of aluminum for nuclear proliferation."*

Andre looked over his shoulder to all six staring in his direction.

:

September 13th

"You going to eat that?" asked John, pointing to the last piece of skewered lamb on Irish's plate.

"No. You go ahead," said Irish as he looked to the televised soccer match on the other side of the café.

"How come you never went for that pimp's phone number when Bain offered it?"

"Are you rubbing it in my face that you're getting laid and I'm not, you son of a bitch. Look how much more you have to eat, laying siege to my plate to fuel your cock."

John laughed and almost choked. "No. It's just...."

"Can it Johnny. I didn't have to be a translator to understand last week's local news story."

"The one about the distressed father who shot up the local brothel to rescue his daughter?"

"Yeah, that's the one. And another thing, did you see how fast that degenerate, Andre, rushed for that pimp's number? I don't want to be anywhere the fuck he is. I'd like to believe when this is all over, I can make it home in one piece and without the clap. In the meantime, I will just do the daily stroke."

"Gotcha." John thought for a moment and asked, "What do you miss about home?"

"Besides pussy, whose father won't shoot me?"

"Yeah. Besides that."

"Family, obviously."

"Obviously. But what else?"

"I miss the ocean. God, I miss the ocean. *My type* of coffee, *my type* of tea, my food. This stuff is good

133

but...." Irish shook his head. "I miss better alcohol. I yearn for a Guinness."

"Is that everything?"

"Ummm. No. I miss rock-n-roll and the blues. My Rory Gallagher cd collection."

"Don't know him. Gary Moore kinda stuff?"
Irish gave a wry smile. "Yes, sort of like Gary Moore. How do you know about that Johnny?"

"I had a white friend once."
Irish laughed. "Oh, very sweet of you to take one of us Caucasians in."

"I do what I can for *you* people."

"Very nice. So, what do you miss?"

"I miss the ocean too, the seasons, Italian food and pastries."

"Ah yes."

The soccer broadcast was interrupted, and a patron pointed, shouting to make the TV louder.
On the screen, President Bush addressed the United Nations on the possession of weapons of mass destruction by the Iraqi government.

Irish, staring at the TV, swallowed the lump in his throat. "Bain was right. This is it," he said in a whisper.
John took a sip of coffee, pretending not to notice a few of the men in the room looking over to the English-speaking foreigners in the room. He looked up to the TV. "Yeah. Shit."

"John. I'm going to have to make another phone call."

.
.

"I am sorry Sir. There is no getting through to Cork at this moment, due to problems with either cables or satellite transmission. You may try back later."

"Thank yo…."

CLICK

"Did you hear that, partner?"

A hundred odd miles away from the desert highway pay phone, Irish fought back tears in his apartment, pausing to set his voice. *"Sigh*….Yeah. These things happen. Thanks for making the trip."

"Never a problem."

"We'll try again soon. Bring it back to town. I got dinner tonight."

CHAPTER
FIFTEEN

Midday-

John stood out front of the clinic. Irish pulled up and the two drove off.

Irish's voice filled with anxiousness. "Wow. He called to get you ready?"

"Yeah. Must be important." John looked around. "Where we going?"

"To an apartment on the south side. Is your pretty boss mad you leaving early?"

"Fire me."

:

Irish and John pulled up to an old, dumpy, unattached building in a lower-class neighborhood. It was a multi-family dwelling with four apartments per floor, though all were empty judging from the outside, where the vacancy was visible through the window bars. On the third floor, Tino answered at the second door on the right. Both men walked to the kitchen, where Bain shuffled paperwork. "Just a minute," he grumbled.

Irish looked to John and rolled his eyes. "I gotta take a leak."

John remained in the kitchen at the end of the table staring at Bain, who didn't yet look up.

"Oh shit!" exclaimed Irish loud enough to be heard in the next room.

In the bathtub Andre and Tino removed the clothes from a throat-cut corpse of a man in his late twenties for dismemberment. John looked over Irish's shoulder, keeping a straight face. Andre looked to Irish standing horrified in front of the toilet. "What's your problem?"

"I gotta take a piss."

"So, take a fucking piss!"

Irish unzipped as John walked back to the kitchen, where Bain still sat not looking up. "So, who was he?"

In the bathroom Irish grimaced from the sound of sawing bone as he tried to relieve himself.

After a moment Bain looked up. "He was following me around. When they're done bagging him, I want you to dump him all around town." Bain then looked back to his paperwork as Irish returned to the kitchen.

John knew that was his dismissal, but remained stationary. "I thought these services were paid for."

Bain stopped writing. "This one I'm keeping on the down low," he said with a building undertone of aggravation. He continued writing. "I got contacts to make."

"What are we doing?" asked Irish, still clueless to the assignment.

Andre walked over, still with rubber gloves on and a big smile. "He's ready."

"Ah shit."

137

Later that night Irish sat in his car with the engine running as he nervously checked all three mirrors.

John got in. "That's the last of him. Drive me home."

Irish sped off. A mile passed before he asked, "You can sleep? I need a drink." John didn't reply. He leaned against the door with his foot on the dash. After a moment of thought, Irish continued, "Why is someone following him?"

John looked over to Irish then back ahead.

Irish fished for a response, "Aren't you pissed off?"

"Of course I'm pissed, but it's been a long day and drinking will just make it longer."

As they pulled up to John's building, a man came out supporting a pregnant woman. The man helped her to take a seat on the entrance steps and started to run over to Irish's car.

"Hey, man, you know this guy?"

"My neighbor. What the...."

Irish rolled down the window for the approaching man.

"My niece is about to give birth," he said in clear English "Please get us to the hospital."

"Yeah, sure," Irish responded, quick, but uneasy.

The man helped the girl from the steps to the car. As she passed in front, the beams of the headlights revealed blood on her dress.

"Shit!" exclaimed John.

"Why is she bleeding so much?" asked Irish.

John grabbed the flashlight from the glove box and got out to help the girl into the back seat. "I used to be a EMT," he said to the man, who then looked back confused. "Emergency Medical Technician." The neighbor nodded and sat up front with Irish as John sat in back. "I have medical experience. What is your name?" he asked in Arabic.

138

"Asera. I speak English."

"Asera, I need to look."

Asera looked to her uncle for approval. "Show him," he said without hesitation.

The young girl revealed a statistical 1% pregnancy nightmare, UCP -umbilical cord prolapse.

"Almost there? We got a problem. We gotta move it."

Irish quickly weaved through traffic. "Almost."

"Asera, I need you to put your elbows to your knees."

"Why? What are you going to do?"

John did his best to keep his voice steady and words pronounced to appear confident, if not for the woman, at least for himself. For he was well aware of the 40% mortality of the medical condition outside of a medical facility. Twice as an EMT in Upper Manhattan, he had rushed to peoples' apartments during the same complication, running up the stairs of buildings without elevators, each time being too late.

"It's called UPC. Your umbilical cord came out with the breaking of the water. If we don't push the baby and the cord back...."

"Uncle Gabir!"

"Asera, please!" snapped Gabir.

"If I don't push the cord and baby back, it will choke from the pressure on the cord." Irish drove around traffic at a light as Asera brought her elbows to her knees, allowing John to proceed.

"I see the hospital." Irish looked over the seat. "Oh my God! What the fuck are you doing?"

"One block," shouted Gabir.

Irish came screeching and beeping into the emergency entrance of the hospital, alerting security. Upon the car stopping, Gabir jumped out and ran into the building, shouting for a gurney.

．
．

Around 1:00 a.m. Gabir entered the hospital waiting area where Irish and John reclined on chairs half asleep. John postured up. "So, what's the news?"

"A healthy girl."

"Congratulations. You're now a granduncle," said Irish with a yawn.

"I want to thank you both. You for you quick thinking, and you for your quick eh….cowboy driving." Gabir laughed with the young men, unaware that their laughter was part sleep deprived and part bewildered by the ups and downs of the day. A day starting with death and ending in birth.

"Asera's husband is in her room now, so we can go tell the good news. I got a surprise for you both."

．
．

2:00 a.m.

Back at Gabir's apartment, he placed down a bottle of booze on to the dining room table joining the assortment of traditional dishes. John and Irish recognized the traditional Iraqi bryani, basmati rice with spicy lamb balls, tepsi baytinijan, a tomato based casserole with meat, onions and eggplant. Everything smelled delicious and Irish and John enjoyed some of each dish. Two young girls were in the kitchen preparing more food and cleaning pots.

Irish reached for the bottle. "Wow. Thirty-year-old scotch. Just when I thought I was out of surprises."

Gabir started to pour for the three of them. "I got this long ago when I went to England for two years of college."

John reached for his glass. "How long ago did you want a drink?"

"Yeah right," Irish said, laughing, "I don't think I'm getting to work tomorrow. Fire me."

John looked over with a smile as the host poured for the first round. "I believe it to be a legitimate sick day."

While pouring, Gabir added, "Yes. Life is too short to work it away."

As the drinking commenced, Gabir pulled out three cigars.

One of the young girls brought over another plate of food. "Uncle Gabir. You're not going to smoke that in the apartment, are you?"

"Well, I'm not going to eat it."

The girl rolled her eyes and returned to the kitchen.

"Hey!" Gabir yelled toward the kitchen as the young girl walked away. "Once the baby is here, I can never smoke again!" he yelled.

John smiled. "You taught them English well."

"Yes, they know how to complain in two languages very well. If I don't have money, at least they can inherit knowledge."

Gabir patted his pockets for a light. "Hold on, I'll get a light," he said, as he got up to go to the kitchen.

John reached for one of the cigars. "Wow. Fucken Cubans."

Irish looked to John with a grin. "Why? Are they illegal in Canada too?"

John looked up suddenly.

"Gotcha yank."

John threw back a swig as Gabir returned, lighting all three cigars.

Irish reclined back in a puff of smoke. "Not bad."

There was silence, a moment of reflection taken by each.

Gabir leaned in to take a drink, after which he paused, staring at his cigar. "Despite all I've been through, I still feel blessed. I left college to fight in the war with Iran to defend my country, or so I was told," he said, finishing with a shrug of his shoulders. "In any event, after the war, the economy was in bad shape. My brother lost a leg in the fighting, so he could no longer do his construction job." He took a deep breath. "Out of money. With the little military benefits he received, he moved into my old apartment with his wife. I had just gotten married. It was the four of us, and we were never closer. We played games together, went out together, so much fun."

John and Irish listened nervously, knowing that somewhere in this story there has to be tragedy.

"My wife and I had two boys. My brother and his wife had the three beautiful girls you met tonight. As crowded as it was, it was crowded with love."

John and Irish sat silent, captivated and nervously anticipating the worst; and then it came.

"The bombing of 1990 killed my two sons, my wife, my brother and his wife, bringing our family unit from nine to four. *Sigh*....Asera, as young as she was, helped me raise her two younger sisters. It was hard at the beginning, but still love survived. Asera got married. Four became five and tonight five became six." Gabir paused and smiled. "So, I am again crowded with love."

The young men nodded meekly. Irish took a long drag.

"That is my first blessing, family. My second is good neighbors and friends."

Gabir raised his glass to toast. John and Irish followed suit as the front door opened and two tall, muscularly lean soldiers walked in. Surprised, they looked up suddenly, but still kept cool. Irish pounded down the drink.

Gabir jumped from his seat. "Oh, Malik, meet the men who saved your wife and baby's lives."

Malik and the other soldier appeared to be midranking officers with decorated uniforms and berets.

"My wife has told me everything," he said in clear English. "I want to thank you both."

Irish and John exchanged the usual pleasantries with the two soldiers, who shook hands a little too tight as they looked them up and down. They expressed the demeanor of steely emotionless men still on duty.

Irish was the first to initiate escape. "It's late and we've had a long day."

Malik returned a closed smile and nod. "I am sure."

After a quick awkward goodbye, both men walked across the hallway. With Gabir's door now closed behind them, without a word they looked to each-other, acknowledging the sense of relief.

"John. I'm too drunk to drive in this town."

"Come on in."

⋮

The next morning Irish and John stood on either side of Irish's car looking through the open back doors. The back seat resembled a bloody crime scene. Both men's noses crinkled from the smell.

"Walking to breakfast?" suggested John.

Irish slammed the door shut. "You're buying me another car."

"Fine," John said, shutting the door.

Both men walked up the street to a very popular bakery café. Both men ate, silence between them, until John spoke. "I'm still taking it all in."

"I'm not ready to talk about it either."

John watched Irish devouring his breakfast, shoveling a fork topped with spinach omelet in one hand while simultaneously dipping flat-bread into thick buffalo cream, ready to jam his face again quickly after. John asked, "Is that the table etiquette you're taught in your corner of the British Empire?"

Irish quickly swallowed and shot back, "Fuck you! It's one island, one country. Always has been, always fucking will be!"

John leaned in with a smile, "Gotcha, you mick IRA fuck."

Irish shut his eyes and sighed at the payback. He then looked up to John eating with a grin. "Asshole. You only got me cause I'm hungover."

John smirked back, then glanced over Irish's shoulder to see Harry walk in. "Hey look who came out for grub."

Irish looked over. "Oh, he's going to be pissed we got here first."

Getting closer, Harry spotted them both and rolled his eyes.

"Relax Harry," John shouted in Spanish over the noise of the hustle and bustle. "Pull up a chair."

"What's one more?" declared Irish.

"I thought I was the only one who knew about the good food here." Harry joined them at the table and started to dig into John's food, dipping the flatbread into the date syrup.

"What do you say Harry? Bend the rules, hang with us from now on?"

"Yeah, they can't fire you," insisted Irish for the sake of continuing the inside joke.

Harry nodded, with a mouth full of food, and took a healthy gulp of coffee.

"You guys look like shit. What happened last night?"

John and Irish grinned at each other and proceeded to
fill Harry in on the marathon day.

CHAPTER
SIXTEEN

"English speaking operator please." The beeping went on for roughly only five minutes. But they were long minutes of expectancy of disappointment. Irish scanned the desert and scrutinized each oncoming blur coming over the horizon for police lights. *What would I tell the police if they asked me questions anyway?* It didn't matter. Irish wasn't going to ask John to drive a hundred or more miles again for a TV-type *-Sorry, we're experiencing technical difficulties-* scenario.

The beeping stopped, followed by the English-speaking operator.
The fear of disappointment vanished when Brendan picked up.
And the anxiety started when he heard the ring of his ex's phone.

"Shannon."

"Oh, hi. Long time no hear."

"Please Shannon. I've had a rough couple of days. I tried calling you on the thirteenth of last month and the phones were fucked up. Everything here is dog shit! You have no idea what this place is like."

Shannon was silent.

"Hello?"

"I was letting you talk."

"Well, do something commutative. Something normal, like... *Right*, *I Know*, or even *Uh-huh*."

"Did you call to yell at me?"

Irish paused, closed his eyes and took a breath. "No. No, I didn't. How are you and the girls?"

"We're good. The girls are in school and getting along. Still no word on citizenship yet."

"Paper-work moves slow in every country."

"Well, I don't know if it's the paperwork."

"What do you mean?"

"Deposit please...."

"Shit! Hold on Shannon."

"Thank you"

"Still there?"

"This local councilman that your uncle knows. He stopped by the house. Said he was waiting on a few things to come through. So, it's obvious it's about money. So sneaky looking. I did not like him at all."

"Ok. Just hang in there."

"Do I have a choice?"

He knew better than to respond to the rhetorical question. He also felt that speaking any further on the subject would shed more light to the harsh reality that he could do nothing to help until the job was done and he picked up his money in Dubai. "Let me say hello to the little ones."

"Ok."

Shannon called for the girls. Irish could tell that she put the phone to her chest, as the conversation between them was inaudible. The girls came to the phone, but were not as talkative and when asked about school, responded with one-word answers. He sent them kisses and Shannon came back on line.

He asked, "So, what's with the teenage attitudes?"

"It isn't teenage attitudes. I tore them away from the show they were watching."

"A show? Are you fucking kidding me?"

"They're kids, Daniel. For Christ's sake! I still have to wipe their noses. They are still babies. You're out of sight and out of mind. What do you expect of them? They have no concept of time."

"Deposit please...."

"Hold on."

"No, save your money. If *I* don't or can't understand what you're going through, do you think *they* will? Please call us next time with a level head."

"I'm sorry Shannon."

CLICK

CHAPTER
SEVENTEEN

October 11ᵗʰ-

Early morning, Sue hurried down the busy avenue, weaving through the local merchants just setting up their tables outside the storefronts. She stopped in her tracks and turned upon hearing a paper-boy on a street corner shouting in Arabic the day's headline:

"US Congress passes joint resolution to authorize military."

John was already at the clinic, in his cubicle filling out paperwork, when Sue came through the door waving the paper.

"Have you been paying attention to this?"
John, behind the partition, swallowed the lump in his throat. "Attention to what?" he asked, while staying hidden.

"The newspaper. Little boy Bush is pushing for another war with Saddam."
John paused for thought with eyes wrenched closed before he stood up. "You bought that paper, right?"

"Yeah?"

"Well, that was why you bought it. Because that stupid shit sells papers. Don't wrap your head up with that hype. You have enough people here to deal with.

Read this instead," he said, exchanging four inches of files for the newspaper.

John walked back to the cubicle as Sue let out a sigh, diving immediately into the files.

"Yeah, you're probably right."

He stole a quick glance back to Sue as he slid the newspaper under his sweatshirt to be smuggled out later and thrown in the trash can at the corner.

CHAPTER
EIGHTEEN

November 14th

John worked at his desk when Anna approached. "What happened to our scheduled delivery?" she asked with an undertone of worry.

John's phone rang. "I don't know where Louis is. I'll make some calls. Just a minute." John answered the phone as Anna walked away in a huff.

Bain was on the line. "I've already told the other guys not to drive the route. Have you noticed anybody strange hanging around your job?"

John walked to the front and peered out the window. "No. I haven't."

"Go straight home after work and wait for Patrick. Make sure you're not followed."

CLICK

John trudged back to his cubicle, flopped into his chair and leaned back. "Shit."

:

Bain's House-

Harry, John and Irish sat awkwardly staggered from Tino in the kitchen for a while in contemplative silence before Bain emerged from the next room with Andre, who remained standing.

"There's some competition in town. Andre is coming with me to the meeting. The four of you will post up at the three cafes across the street."

"Are we getting guns?" asked Irish.

"I don't expect any trouble."

"Then why are we going?"

"To make a show. This is the first of many meetings to work things out."

Irish looked down as Bain continued.

"Nothing is going to happen. There's a large security presence because of the Swiss Embassy nearby."

The Swiss Embassy, located in a busy up-and-coming section of downtown Baghdad has been in the last few years, surrounded by a boom of economic and urban reconstruction. New hotels were built to accommodate foreign business, businesses forecasted by economists both local and international to be on the rise. New apartments, entertainment, and dinning were built as a collaboration between the government and the private sector for the emerging professional class, with newly modest, but disposable income.

First Café-

Harry walked in cautiously and took a seat across from three white men speaking French, who quickly took notice of the tall dark stranger. Harry reclined against a wall in a booth directly across from them and looked over.

Second Café-

Tino walked to a table of four white men. Upon seeing the approaching thug, the men quieted. One of the men slowly removed a knife from the table and concealed it underneath. Tino, sneering at the men, took a long drag of his cigarette and flicked it down at the end of the table. Confidently and arrogantly, he turned his back to the men, sat at the counter and ordered a coffee, of which he poured his flask into.

Third Café-
John and Irish entered the café as locals trickled in after the evening meal in which the daily fast is broken during the month-long holiday of Ramadan. They took seats and ordered coffees. Diagonally across was a table of four white men, beyond them, a TV showed the news.
The cups were placed before them at the small table.
Irish leaned in to whisper, keeping his eyes on the French men. "Yeah. He doesn't expect trouble. I swear to God, I'm gonna get us our own fucking guns."

"Shushh….Shut the fuck up."

"What if something goes wrong? What are we supposed to do?"

"*Sigh*…. Apparently just make a phone call."
Irish pulled out a flask and added to the coffee.

"What the fuck? You too?"
Irish quickly met his eyes and spoke with a strong, but hushed tone, "Don't give me that *you too* shit. I'm not Bain or Tino and I'm not smoking hash or shooting up."
John didn't reply.

"Shitty country gets to me sometimes. That's all."

Hotel Room-
The room door opened and the man turned his back with no greeting. Bain and Andre walked in. There was a small exchange of French among the crew. The leader of the French team, known and addressed by his team as only the "Captain," sat at a table with three of his

153

men standing about. Bain took a seat across from the man. Andre cautiously posted up, leaning against a wall behind.

"Small crowd. Where are the Russians?" Bain asked with sarcasm, knowing the answer.

"They left," responded the Captain coolly. It was his order to put the bomb under the car while the four men had been dining out their first week in the city, never aware it was their last meal. "Where are the Austrians?"

Andre looked over to Bain. It was Andre who had dressed as a Shia woman and riddled those three men sipping coffee on a street corner.

"They left too," Bain said with a smirk.
The Captain leaned back and nodded with a short smile.

Bain was the first to break through the BS. "Can we agree that if this shit keeps up, the government is going to crack down on *all* foreigners?"

"Agreed. Let's talk of the divisions." With a gesture, a file was brought to the table. Bain reached for his glasses and opened the file.

First Café-
Harry, still staring in imitation of the men across from him, had enough, "Go fuck yourselves," he said calmly in French.

Third Café-
John and Irish's eyes darted between the men at the table and the window. On the TV, a report of Iraq's agreement six days earlier to United Nation's Resolution 1441- allowing inspections of the weapons disarmament process to resume unhindered, 45 days from the signing, re-establishing the predominant

compliance of Resolution 687 of 1991, which called for the removal and destruction of all chemical and biological weapons and any ballistic missiles with a range greater than 150 kilometers. Adhered to this was the Security Council's request of locations of said material within 15 days.

One of the men at the table turned around. "Maybe we can all go home soon," he said in English.
John was shocked frozen to see it was Louis, the truck driver from work. John kept cool, not letting Irish in on the delicateness of the situation.
"Do you really think so?"

Hotel Room-
Bain flipped through the file of artifact photos. "Where are the tablets?"
"The tablets are not an option. What else do you want?"
"I want what the boss wants."
"Then we both have to talk with our bosses."

Third Café-
John and Irish stared at Louis.
Louis looked back to the TV and shrugged his shoulders. "Or maybe not."
Remy, coming from the bathroom, joined the men at the table.
John's and Irish's phones each rang. Getting up to leave, both pushed themselves from the tables slowly, as not to alarm the other men. They walked with intermittent glances over their shoulders to the door

.
.

Later that week another meeting at Bain's had Irish and John walking down the garbage alley to the house and past the posted goons who guarded Bain's house. The other three of the crew were already present.

Upon their entrance, Bain went right into a mission update. "A couple of you have already lost your jobs and the rest of you will probably lose yours' soon with all the shit going on. Stay out of trouble. Don't drive too much, if you do, obey all the traffic laws. They're pulling a lot of people over now. I know Resolution 1441 has been in the news celebrating the diversion of war. It does not give Iraq enough time to destroy said weapons or disclose all that is specified. Saddam is trying to buy time, hoping the United States will lose ground in Afghanistan, putting this place on the back shelf."

John and Irish drove away, mentally exhausted, in silence. The rest of Bain's villain pep talk played over in their heads. *"The hawks in Washington won't let this happen. This war is still on, but it's off until the last two weeks in March. For this, you all get another twenty percent."*

CHAPTER
NINETEEN

Irish, with grocery bags in hand, stared at his apartment door. The white spray paint graffiti looked fresh on the brown backdrop. "What the fuck?" he murmured, as he fumbled for the keys, trying not to drop the groceries. From behind he heard, "Merry Christmas." Startled, he quickly turned to see his elderly woman neighbor.

"Excuse me?"

"Merry Christmas," she said with a wide smile. "It is your holy day, is it not?"

"Ah, yes. Thank you very much."

The elderly woman reached for her door handle when Irish asked, pointing to his door, "Oh, Miss...." She turned. "What does this say?"

She leaned to her right and looked around him. "Only foolish things of children." With that she entered her apartment.

Within an hour Irish met up with Harry and John at a café, where both sat facing the street, relaxing and taking the sun on a clear day.

"Did you guys know it was Christmas?"

John and Harry looked up, then to each other.

Harry broke into laughter. "Ooh, we've been here way too long."

John sat up. "Wow. No. Ramadan just ended and aside from the restaurants shut until sunset, who can tell around here? People still go to work. The last time you could tell it was a holiday was Saddam's birthday."

Harry interjected, "A lovely parade," he said, rolling his eyes.

John noticed Irish's contemplation as he looked out to the street. John shot a look to Harry, who was just shaking off the laughter. Harry, sensing the awkwardness, straightened up.

"Did Sue say anything?" asked Irish.

"She's a Buddhist in a Muslim country, so it's not really in her face and she's pretty preoccupied with the scarcities at the clinic."

Irish nodded in understanding.

"Take a seat man. You ok?"

"Yeah sure. It was just very sobering, that's all." Irish grabbed a chair. "We have been here too long."

"No religious guilt?" asked John with a smile.

"No no no." Irish started to lighten up.

"You sure? Because there's a English service down the street."

"Fuck you dick," responded Irish with a laugh.

Each contemplated in the moment of silence, as the three men looked out to the traffic on the street.

"John. You a believer?" asked Irish in a soft, but serious tone.

"In Jesus. Yeah."

"What about you, Harry?"

"Yeah. But I don't think that matters anymore."

Irish's disposition became immediately defensive. "Harry, even if we were to scream the inevitable from the rooftops, no one would believe it."

"Is that how you rationalize it? Is that how you sleep at night?"

"Fuck you Harry! Who do you think...."

John cut in. "Whoa, whoa….relax. I think this shit is eating us all."

All was quiet for a moment with Irish and Harry looking in opposite directions. John continued, "He's right, Harry, no one would believe us."

"I know that. And I'm here to do a job and I'm going to do it." Harry paused for a moment. "We're stealing culture," he said calmly.

"Pieces of stone!' snapped Irish. "It's not the fucking Sphinx, Harry!"

"We're stealing culture," repeated Harry again, unchanged in tone.

"No, we're *saving* culture. If it stays here, it will be blown to bits anyway. Look at how much was lost during the Nazi bombing of the Acropolis in Greece. We're *saving* culture."

"We're robbing these people's identity. Something that proves to the world's future generations that there was something here before Saddam, the Brits, or the Turks. But hey, *fuck it*, as you two say. We got a job to do, right?"

The three men looked back out to the traffic, silence between them until John spoke, "What if we don't?"

"Don't what?" asked Irish with agitation in his voice. "Finish the mission? I'm not ruining the reputation of the man who sent me here."

"And what good will you be to that person whose reputation you're so concerned about if you're dead?"

Irish stared straight ahead, unresponsive.

"Harry? What do you say? Had enough?"

Harry, who also pensively stared out to the street, nodded.

John stood and spoke in a strong, but hushed tone, "Good. Let's get the hell out of here. We can run back to our apartments, grab our hidden cash and be at the

airport in an hour to *anywhere,* but here." Looking directly at Irish, John asked, "Come on partner. Let's get the fuck out of this place."
Irish finally made eye contact and nodded.

"We have got to make one last trip first," said Harry.
Both men turned inquisitively.

"Trust me."

.
.

Harry insisted John ride passenger with him and lead the way, followed by Irish separately to a warehouse section east of downtown Baghdad. It was a large drab building without windows and similar to the others surrounding it, except for many empty parking spots in front and on the sides during the middle of a workday. Harry, the first to park, got out with John and walked to the front of the building, followed by Irish.

John froze upon seeing the sign above the entrance. Below it, Harry stood, holding open the door until a security guard just on the inside asked him to either enter or exit.
Walking up the path behind, Irish asked, "What is this place?"

"The morgue," said John, not looking back as he went for the door.

As expected, the building was cold. The hallway was long and they could see the warehouse space just above the eight-foot wall on either side, with joined second-story mezzanines of steel girders and catwalks between storage compartments. At the end of the hall, on the other side of a sliding glass window, a man of around sixty sat at a desk in a florescent lit, temperature

160

controlled office. Harry spoke in Arabic and gestured to Irish. The man looked to Irish, but continued addressing Harry with palms up and a shrug of his shoulders. Harry discreetly reached into his pocket and slid a thousand dinars through the window. The man looked to the calendar behind and nodded.

Irish's eyes darted between the man behind the glass and Harry.

"We will see now," said Harry, quietly, more to himself than Irish or John.

A different man in a lab coat came out of the office area and led the three men into the 2nd story storage mezzanine, stopping at unit 208.

It happened so fast, the cab driver and his passenger never had a chance. It was five hundred feet to the last red traffic light on International Airport Road, where conservative women from the poorer surrounding neighborhoods, clothed in full black abaya with faces veiled, walked up and down the median between the oncoming traffic. For the few dinars a day, they peddled bottled water and za'atar, a small flat-bread, baked with a thyme based spice mixture, to those caught at the traffic lights and congestion backing up from the terminals.

Alongside traffic, two men in full women's garb walked with heavy, unbalanced baskets to the taxi, where each pulled an Uzi from within their baskets and fired until the clips were nearly empty. As chaos ensued, with people making failed attempts at driving around the vehicle in front, haphazardly jumping out onto the pavement, or just crouching down, a small brown BMW, coming from the airport with two men in front, pulled alongside the other side of the divider. The assassins jumped over the divider, into the back seats and sped away.

Harry whispered to Irish, "Be cool. I told him you were looking for your brother who disappeared."

The man reached for the handle, pulled, and out slid the unclothed body of a Caucasian male in his late forties with blond hair streaked with blood.

Irish stood stone cold, looking down upon the body.

John asked in Spanish, "Is it him?"

Harry looked back down to the body covered only by a sheet. "Even with his face filled with bullet holes it appears so. And his arrival matches the day he was on his way to the airport."

"Where are his clothes?" John asked the coroner in Arabic. And to Harry in Spanish, he asked, "You would recognize his clothes?"

Harry looked to John and Irish. "We have to be honest with ourselves." In Spanish he continued, "It is Mike."

The coroner fidgeted, obviously uncomfortable with talking to the three foreigners, looked down at the floor as he talked. "The police are supposed to keep it for forensics. With crime rising due to the current situation, I could not tell you how much time they devoted. I am sure they have closed the file by now and declared this to be another unsolved crime. He is scheduled to be cremated next week if no one claims him."

Harry, in a deliberate display of a bribe, counting out dinars, he asked "Do you remember any details from the police report?"

The coroner with eyes on the money, answered, "He was on the way to the airport."

Harry stopped counting the bills and paused for effect. "If he was on his way to the airport, I'm sure you have a cab driver here that came in on the same day. What do you remember of *his* report? This is not your typical crime. Where were they coming from?"

"Taxi picked him up from Yafa Street."

Harry shed a slight smile knowing that Yafa Street was near the Telecommunications and Post Company office. Now secure that Mike sent a letter home to someone with information on the cash account, he gave all the peeled dinars to the coroner and leaned into Irish, whispering, "Just shake your head no."

Irish, trance-like, complied, prompting the coroner to pull the sheet over the head and slide the unidentified man back into the unit and return to his regular duties.

Harry turned to John and Irish, who stood staring at unit 208. "I think we have seen enough."

Irish looked up and whispered, "Leaving is not going to be easy."

John looked to his partners and spoke in a strong, but hushed tone, "Let's get whatever we have, hit the airport and go anywhere, like I said before."

"Let's talk about it back at our cars," Harry quickly answered, at the same time giving a subtle look to Irish, who was about to reply.

All three men arrived back at the café and stood before their vehicles.

Harry spoke, shooting a quick glance to Irish, "Let's go home, count our money, rest on it and discuss our options tomorrow."

Irish and John agreed, and each went his separate way.

.
.

That night Irish peeked through the peephole to see the unexpected visitor. "Evening, Harry. Where's Johnny boy?"

"Solo," he said, entering.

163

Irish's smile disappeared. "I knew there was more bad news." Irish grabbed two beers from the refrigerator and sat across from Harry at the kitchen table. "Ok. Give it to me straight," he said, passing one bottle across to Harry, who refused with a wave of his hand.

"I was just at John's and found a tracking device under his car."

Irish caught, before it crossed his lips, his first reaction of *What the fuck!* Instead, he paused for thought and reached across for the other bottle. "Well, I guess I'll be drinking this one too tonight." After a long swig, Irish asked in an annoyed, hushed tone, "Should we not have stepped outside to have this conversation or at least turned on some music?"

"I checked both of our cars and we are clean."

Irish understood that since a tracker on a car is the first and easiest method of surveillance, that would have been there long before an apartment plant of an audio bug. Irish nodded.

"I didn't remove it. No reason to let Bain know that we know."

"How long did it look like it was there?"

"It did have some grease and road dust on it, but I'd say not long. It was plastic wrapped and tied with wire to the top of a sway bar. It's a simple one that takes a AA battery that has to be replaced every couple of weeks. I did however, see what looked like previous tie-wire marks."

To Irish, Harry's strange insistence on John riding shotgun earlier was now evidently clear. "So, you think it was Bain?"

"I believe so."

"I knew there was bad news with that look you gave me at the morgue. Shit."

Harry leaned in. "Then you likely knew John is not like us. We came highly recommended by organizations or agencies. Aside from combat experience, I think this is his first go of a freelance assignment and Bain does not trust him because he was probably forced into this. Remember when we all first got our envelopes and Bain said to John that he was only getting spending money and that John *knew why*? And Andre made a comment that he must have *screwed up*?"

"I do, and I called him on it. Says they're paid off, and I left it alone. Truth is we're all here for screwing up somewhere, are we not?
Harry made no comment at the rhetorical question.

Irish continued, "When it all comes down to it, they know how much time John and his boss spend together and where she lives."

"Exactly. A woman who operates a neighborhood clinic with children coming and going. Who knows what these people are capable of doing? Perhaps shoot the whole place up." Harry leaned back. "And that is why I am staying."

"Don't bring up children, Harry. If the U.S. Air Force does another firework display in this city like they did eleven years ago, there's going to be kids dying in this city no matter what we do."

"Well, this at least I can make a difference in."
Irish looked directly at Harry. His thoughts raced between how much he missed his daughters, John and Sue's safety, the kids at the clinic, Harry's not so subtle look for a commitment, back to his daughters' college fund of zero before he arrived and then Megan at the Raven's Head. He put down the first bottle, now empty. "You're right. This we can make a difference in. I'm not going to be responsible for any more death than what's already on the way. And I have a lot more money to make." "*Sigh....* So, I will presume this will be our little secret."

"Better that way. Don't you think?"

165

"Yes, but do you think he will really believe that we're going to stay for the money?"

"We could just say it's not worth the risk, that they are going to get at least one of us. So, there is safety in numbers and we might as well ride this to the end."

Irish again thought long and hard. It sounded true, and upon further thought, it actually could be a grave reality. "Sounds more truth than lie."

"In some respects, it could very well be."

"Seems you've pondered all this for a while now. You're a wise old fucker, aren't you Harry."

Harry gave a slight smile. "I would be flattered under normal circumstances."

After a moment of silence between the two, "Sorry about your partner."

Harry nodded in return.

"Did you get to know him?"

"In the end I got a eh….peek to…."

"Glimpse into his personality?"

"Yes, yes a glimpse. We had our disagreements, but that did not stop some laughing over meals out. But his last night here he opened up. What we discovered today, along with the information he relayed in our last conversation, he looked out for me, *for us*. He would have made a good asset to have. On a personal level, I feel there was more good in him than bad."

"Think he had a family?"

"He would never have told me, but I have this feeling that he did. Seems he was coming from an area by the main mailing station"

"Good." Irish tipped back the beer and put down the now second bottle to the table, empty. "Ok then. So be it."

"We will tell John in the morning."

166

：

At the café the next morning, after an explanation, all went as Harry and Irish expected.

"If you guys are staying, then I'm staying."

CHAPTER
TWENTY

Unlike those of its U.S. and European counterparts, the ornate chandeliers in the historic Orthodox Armenian Church of Saint Ibrahim of Arazd were not lit by flame shaped bulbs, but rather real candles, adding to the foreign antiquity of the 400-year-old tile frescoes of the resurrection. On the east side of the Tigris river between the neighborhoods of I'lam and Dawra, in the small mixed Christian enclave of Athuriyin, the service went on in Arabic as not to raise suspicion in the atmosphere of spy paranoia and its following security measures that any Iraqi citizen can be sure will grow intrusive, weaving its way into both secular and religious institutions.

On an early afternoon, Sue and John peeked through the tall, heavy, bronze fastened and decorated wooden doors, seeing Irish, who sat alone and uncomfortable, far from the regular parishioners, comprised mostly of the elderly and homeless. John left Sue out front, joining Irish with a nudge of the arm.

"I knew you were coming," he said quietly with a smile.

"How long we been glued at the hip?"

"Right."

168

Irish looked back to the pulpit for a minute, then gestured with his head. "What's he saying?"

"The last supper where Jesus says, *'I give you another commandment, that you love one another.'*
Both sat silent for a moment. "Crazy how we have to be reminded of the most sensible things."

"Yeah, I know."
Outside, Harry arrived, walking up the church steps at a snail's pace.

"Hey, Harry, you going in?" asked Sue.

"*Sigh.*"

"I think it would mean a lot if you were *both* in there."

"Yes yes."
Harry walked to the pew and gave Irish a pat on the back, which was returned with a smile. Harry then looked up to the hanging Jesus with a face of stone.

:

"Merry Christmas, my dear lady."

"*Sigh*....Dear lady, eh? Are you drunk, Daniel?"

"I'm drunk on Christmas cheer."

"I told you to call with your head straight."

"Ahh! It is fucking straight. Put the girls on!"

"They're sleeping."

"Wake them up."

"I'm not waking them up."

"Why not?"

"Because it's 4:00 a.m., and I don't want them to be cranky in church!"
He was struck by surprise. *Fuck! How long have I been drinking?*

"Call tomorrow. If not, I will tell them you called. Merry Christmas."

CLICK

CHAPTER
TWENTY ONE

"Five...four...three...two...one...Happy New Year!" The small crowd in Gabir's apartment toasted with hugs and kisses exchanged.

"Uh oh," said Gabir, turning to the cry of his awakened grandniece. Asera rushed down the hallway to check on her newborn, as would any new mother.

"Bring the baby to the party. She has to eat anyway," said Gabir with the worry-free confidence of a man who raised three children with two left to go and the slur of one who had actually been drinking since the New Year came in for Sidney, Australia and had toasted along with the TV coverage of each major international city thereafter.

Asera emerged from the room bottle feeding the baby. There were oohs and ahs from those clamoring about the baby girl, two being Irish and Sue.
Gabir's youngest niece answered the apartment phone. "Asera. Malik is on the phone."

"Malik is away on maneuvers," whispered Gabir to John.
Asera looked to Sue. "Would you feed her?"

"Oh, I'd love to."
Asera handed off the baby to Sue and darted off to take her husband's call.

John smiled as he watched Sue's business-free nurturing side come out in full display. "Look at you."

"Yeah. Look at me."

Irish stared down to the baby with mouth agape. Asera stretched the phone cord over and tried to get the baby to coo for the father. Upon hanging up with Malik, Asera returned to finish the feeding.

"Now that you're a mom, do you ever think you'll leave Baghdad?" asked Irish.

John and Harry's ears perked up, and each looked over.

"No. I'm a city girl and so is she," she answered with a smile, but puzzled look.

Irish nodded, fixated on the baby. John and Harry looked to each-other then back just in time to see Irish inconspicuously wiping away a tear. The men locked eyes again. Brought back to the reality of the situation, and their friend's deterioration within it. John averted his eyes, swigged his drink, and turned back to Sue with a smile.

.

Later that night, Irish stared at the ceiling. Too drunk to drive and too anxious to sleep. No more loud drunks passing on the street or beeping car horns. The last of the rooftop celebratory gunfire seemed to be over and all was silent except the voice of worry in his head. It was roughly 3:30 a.m., three and a half hours into a new year of unpredictability. He thought about doing the numbers—without the aid of the cell phone calculator—to figure how many hours were left in 2003 to occupy his mind, but thought better of it. *I'm not doing fucking math now. Fuck that!*

He looked over to the bed on the other side of the room, where Sue and John had both flopped drunk on the mattress and fallen asleep in their street clothes. Irish smirked. *Lightweights*, he said to himself, shaking his head.

He grabbed his cell phone and used it as a flashlight to the bathroom, passing Sue's purse sitting on the kitchen counter. There was no second thought; he retrieved her passport from an inside pocket and brought it into the bathroom, where he entered the needed information on his cell phone. Exiting the bathroom, he replaced the passport in the correct pocket, fluffed up the pillow on the floor, and despite a hastily makeshift mattress of blankets and still many haunting thoughts, Irish finally fell asleep with one less thing to think about.

CHAPTER
TWENTY TWO

January 6th

    Bain pulled the envelope from his pocket and walked through the curtain to the private section of the Safwan Lounge, with Andre close behind. He thought of bringing Tino for the sake of being aware of what was spoken around him, and usually did in these meetings, but this time he thought better of it, not wanting to seem paranoid, or worse, *fearful.*

The Dulamimi crime family, whose tentacles were intertwined with local police, military and politics, could make him disappear at this meeting regardless of whether he had a bodyguard who could overhear the faint murmuring acrimony that precedes malevolence.

In the corner booth at the end, sat Safa with two men. On the floor, their three-foot hookahs burned at the end of the table. Bain now stood in the coal smoke before them, the old man, his body-guard and the translator he knew would be there.

    "*Ijils.*" said the old man, gesturing for Bain to sit. He spoke to his bodyguard, who then stood and posted up by the curtain through which they entered.

"Please have your associate sit in the booth across so we may talk privately," said the translator.

Bain gave a nod to Andre, who did just that.

The old man smiled and the dialogue began. "It's a new year and you are still here. Why? For our food? For our women?"

"For a continued business relationship, of course." Bain slid the envelope across the table.

The old man took it with a smile. "And how long will this relationship last? You said you are here to rob the undisclosed contents of a undisclosed bank safety deposit box. I did not want to know. Your job is your job. But now, with all the money leaving the country, I find your business here hard to believe."

"Safa, I am just as eager to know why I am here as much as you are. The plans have been changed, but to what I am still unsure. I am awaiting instruction."

Safa looked to the table, took a deep breath and at the exhale looked back to Bain. "You are only a few years my junior. We have been at this game for a very long time. The irony is that you know I am not one to lie to, yet I know that you have to lie to me. So, here we sit, nothing said, so instead I will be the one not to lie."

"Safa…."

"Do not interrupt me."

Bain looked back and forth between Safa and the translator, then nodded.

"I believe you are to hijack a shipment at one of the ports. Those are my ports. Whether it be taking a truck or breaking into a container. I want to know what and when. And of course, be compensated."

Bain was about to speak when Safa continued, "And just for my own insurance, I want three more of these," he said, tapping the envelope. "Before the end of the week."

"Triple?" Bain wanted to argue, but knew it was two things, first, he knew it was more to make up on Dulamimi family losses in his other sectors of business, than a matter of insurance on goods taken from a port heist that, ironically, was never going to happen.

The second, Safa said out loud himself. "I keep the cops and local crooks off your back. You don't get to where I am without knowing people high up in the government. There are dark times on the horizon, and during these times, business costs more, loyalty to me costs more, therefore my loyalty to you costs more." Safa nodded to his translator and the three men exited the booth.

The three men accompanied Bain and Andre back to the curtain entrance. Safa patted Bain on the back with the envelope and spoke with a smile that stayed throughout as the translation was relayed to him, "There is a saying in sports, the mistakes made in extra time are the most expensive."

Bain knew what he meant by the analogy. They had worn out their welcome, times were not what they were and the trickle-down economics of an underworld in recession was pissing on his back.

∶

January 16th through 18th

Protests were held worldwide in opposition to war with Iraq. Some countries had more than one major city involved. The largest demonstrations being Ireland, France, Italy, Germany, Norway, Russia, New Zealand, Argentina, Turkey, Egypt, Japan and Pakistan.

The news of a war in a foreign land can stir emotion in some, although many, when given the option, may brush it off, simply ignoring the front page and flip through, change the channel of the radio or TV, or even reach for a non-political magazine.

By contrast, war in a country to be invaded dominates every medium of media. It's in one's face from rise until slumber. Even a blackout cannot grant the bliss of ignorance. In urban centers, from super-markets to train and bus stations, placards on the streets stare down immediately upon leaving one's doorstep. Common are political speeches, before and during the halftime of soccer games.

However, in the end, it is the obligatory military service that provides the catalyst for paying attention for those who would willfully shut their eyes and ears, if given the opportunity. It could be your own worry or that of a loved one that keeps you glued all day to the radio and then the TV news the minute the workday ends.

It was during this time on TV that peace activists calling themselves "Human Shields" were leaving London for Iraq. Some of the men in the café laughed or shook their heads, as did Harry and John.

Irish is the only one to say what everyone in the room was thinking. "Look at these assholes."

.
.

January 27th

"Iraq has given some access, but there is still undetected material and inability to talk with scientists." -Chairman of the inspectors effort report to the United Nations Security Council

.
.

Irish parked and walked down the block and across the street to his apartment building. Twenty-five feet from the entrance, a bottle smashed before him. In the reaction speed of fear, Irish turned around, then to either side. No one around, he then quickly stepped back, looking up. "Shit," he said under his breath. All the windows were dark and all was silent. "Foolish things of children, eh?" he muttered. Eyes up, he entered his building.

⋮

January 28th
President Bush's State of The Union Address
"The British government has learned that Saddam Hussein recently sought significant quantities of uranium from Africa. Our intelligence sources tell us that he has attempted to purchase high-strength aluminum tubes suitable for nuclear weapons production."

⋮

John walked down the corridor from his office to the alley to receive a shipment. After the truck parked, out came Louis.
"Are you expecting help this time?" asked John.
"No. I just want to talk."
"Do you realize how much trouble we can be in if seen together?"
"Yes, but this is probably the last time we will be able to talk."
John gestured to the rolling back door of the truck. "So, work and talk."

Louis jumped in back of the truck. "There's not going to be another meeting John," he said, moving boxes around.

"Bullshit! These things have to be worked out. There's too much at stake."

"Not this time. Our investors are in very deep. War is coming fast and it's *all or nothing* on both sides."

"We should not be talking."

"If not us, who? We have more bank-roll, which buys us favor. We out-number you."

"Why are you telling me this?"

"Let's just say I was conned into this. Me and Remy. Look John, my captain is ruthless. There were other crews here. Now they're gone. It's best for you and anybody you can convince to jump this ship."

"Whatever. Give me my boxes."

Louis handed John only one box.

"Don't fuck around."

"That's it. Anybody with money or influence has been hoarding medical supplies."

John walked to the back edge of the truck, looking to its contents. "What are in the rest of those boxes?"

"Clothes donations." His eyes narrowed. "Do you really think I would withhold medical supplies? Do you?"

John looked at Louis, the truck and directly back. "No."

"It's all coming to an end soon," he said, pulling shut the rolling door. "I'll be out of a job, and so will you." Louis handed John an invoice and walked to the truck. "I hope you see the writing on the wall and get out of here when the time comes."

"I wish I could," he whispered, walking back to the clinic.

Louis opened the driver door to see Remy in the cab, removing a syringe from his arm. "Now you're doing this shit in my truck! In broad daylight!" he scolded in French, throwing his clip-board to the dash.

"I'm sorry."

Attempting composure, Louis leaned his head back to the seat, shutting his eyes. He thought back to years earlier when he and Remy were partners in Marseille's elite bi-lingual narcotics unit, and how his friend could have succumbed to the same vices he fought to rid France of for years.

Frustrated by department corruption in a city, for decades, titled the heroin and hash gateway to Europe, Louis and Remy retired together at the earliest, devoting their new free time to setting up police watchdog groups throughout the city.

On their way north to meet with federal politicians, it was at the edge of the city limits, when they were pulled over by former colleagues and taken into custody.

In the interrogation room. The pictures taken of their children playing at the park were laid out before them and the ultimatum of the Iraq job given. The former policemen had cut into the profits of the law enforcement criminal nexus and had to payback.

Remy gave Louis his needed pause, after which he nervously asked, "How did it go?"

"Not well."

"Doesn't he get it? They don't have a chance."

Louis leaned forward, starting the truck. "He's like everybody else around here. He doesn't believe in a better future."

.
.

International activists arriving in Iraq presume there will be a substantial influx from the U.S. as well. Unfortunately, government travel restrictions, compounded by the threat of criminal prosecution of sedition, cut the number of new arrivals. Fearing that their numbers are not a sufficient obstacle to an attack, many leave, further shrinking the deterrent to invasion even more, likewise breaking the spirit of others who would stay, creating a vicious deterioration of morale and a cycle of flight from Iraq.

While there are agreements between the Iraqi government and some antiwar organizations that no activists were to be used as shields for military sites, those who are steadfast on remaining grow frustrated by the insistence of the Ministry of the Interior's placement of activists at infrastructure facilities rather than schools and orphanages. The government rationale being that without electrical power plants and oil refineries, there is no way to operate schools, orphanages or -for that matter- hospitals. In the end, few remain staying at their assigned locations.

With all the waiting around, the three passed their nights in hookah cafes. Who could avoid the predictable, but still disappointing news footage of the activists who had called themselves Human Shields leaving Iraq for London.
Irish looked up to the TV, now convinced of his earlier opinion, "Look at these assholes."

CHAPTER
TWENTY THREE

February 5, 2003

The contrast is sharp between the winter of 2001/02 and 2002/03 in downtown Baghdad. At a time of year in the capital when most people with even limited disposable income get out on the town. Many businesses were closed due to the invasion scare, despite the threat of license revocation from the municipal government if they did not remain open.

At one of the few nice restaurants to remain open, John and Sue finished ordering and handed back the menus. The business closures and its resulting unemployment has led to a rise in panhandling at intersections that both pretended not to notice for the sake of non-heavy thought or conversation, but rather just a romantic night.

John tried to turn Sue's pensive look into a smile and squelch the awkwardness. "This is nice," he said, glancing around the ornately decorated restaurant. No immediate response or eye contact. *Shit.* John braced for the jab.

"You think it's nice even though I had to drag you out tonight?"

Jab thrown. "Sue, please," said John as a waiter dropped off tea and a small plate of lahm b'jeen- a small flatbread topped with chopped lamb.

John immediately dug in, part hunger, part not wanting a fight.

"I want to spend as much time with you as I can before we're all kicked out. I wish you felt the same way."

"I do," he replied, midchew, with his hand covering his mouth.

"No you don't," Sue said, slightly raising her voice.

"Really?" John wiped his face and threw his napkin to the table. "I don't believe this shit."

"Maybe I don't believe the three-musketeer story."

"What?"

Sue leaned in and asked with a strong, but hushed tone, "What do your friends do for a living? In detail, please."

John scanned the room nervously. "What kind of question is that?"

"Sometimes, on trips to and from the hospital, I see Harry and Irish sipping drinks in front of a café. I guess waiting for you like two delinquents waiting for the third to cut out of school. What the hell is that?"

"They work off hours."

Sue rolled her eyes, leaning back in her seat as John continued,

"Look. I'm sorry if I haven't been in the mood for female companionship."

Sue sprung up in her seat. "Female companionship? Is that what I am? I'm in this mess too. Walking every day on eggshells. Wondering what will happen next." Sue's composure started to fade as her eyes welled up with tears. "I'm the one turning patients away every day because we lack supplies, and it's killing me. Sometimes

I can use a companion. I don't care, male or female. Shit, John. If I didn't know better…."

"Know what, Sue? Know what?"

Across the restaurant, a patron yelled to make the TV louder. On the screen, Colin Powell spoke at a podium, pointing to satellite photos of supposed poison gas facilities and missile launch sites, making the case for war before the United Nations.

A tear rolled down Sue's cheek. "Oh, these poor people."

John stood and reached for her hand. "Come on babe. We'll get the food to go."

She took his hand, fighting back tears as she stood. "I'm not hungry anymore."

Later that night Sue and John were curled up in bed.

"I'm sorry I snapped tonight."

"Shush. It's all right," said John, kissing her forehead.

"All this talk of war in the last few months has made me feel like all the treatment here was worthless. And that's probably selfish of me. Because I'm making it about me when it's really the people who live here that have the serious problem." She looked up to John's face. "You get it?"

"I get it."

"I feel guilty saying this, but I can't wait for you and me to be on a plane to Canada."

"Yeah, a plane to Canada."

John stared up to the ceiling as Sue closed her eyes, nuzzling next to him.

CHAPTER
TWENTY FOUR

Another meeting at Bain's had Irish and John walking up to the house through the alley in the rain. They looked to the empty spot where the lookouts would usually be, their car nowhere in sight. Each made the mental note, but said nothing of it.

Inside waited the rest of the crew. Both men plopped into seats next to Harry.

Bain began, "We're still looking at the last two weeks of March, but a few things have changed."
John watched Andre walking from window to window, peering out each.
       "Bush is crazier than imagined. The U.S. now wants to occupy Baghdad."
John leaned forward. "How can you occupy a city of millions with a machine gun in every apartment?"

Due to years of war with Iran, the Iraqi government encouraged gun ownership as long as the weapons didn't leave one's house. It was calculated, that advocating for a militia type populace -where most men had done military service and knew how to handle a weapon- was the strongest deterrent to invasion.

"I don't know, but they're going to try."

"It's impossible. They don't have the soldiers to do this," John said adamantly.

Andre sat down, attentively listening.

As a seasoned military officer, Harry knew the sad strategic answer. "They are going to bomb the fighting spirit out of these people. Are they not?"

"Yes," replied Bain coldly. "I can't imagine any other way. That is the logical means to the end they seek, even if one believes the end they seek is illogical or counterproductive."

In the ensuing silence, John shifted in his seat, then spoke. "I don't think you can bomb away these people's fighting spirit."

"Fuck these people," Tino snarled. "You're speaking as if you care."

Andre quickly chimed in with an accusatory tone. "Maybe you been here too long."

"I'm making a point. Maybe you guys have been junkies too long."

Andre's chair kicked out from under him as he stood with fists clenched. "You're making shit!"

John quickly stood with Irish and Harry on one side, with Tino rising behind Andre on the other.

Bain loudly interjected, stopping the would-be brawl. "Hey! We've all been here too long. That's why routes and rendezvous have to change. So pay attention!"

The three men on one side and the two on the other stared at one another as they slowly retook their seats.

Harry asked Bain. "Have you talked to the French yet?"

"No. Not yet"

John took notice, as once again, Andre peered out each window.

"Then these plans could be void," said Harry.

"They could be, but I think we can come to an agreement. Gather around with a pad and pen."

185

At the kitchen table, Bain laid out a map. "This is the new route, and this is the new destination."

"The airport?" asked Irish.

"With all this dragging out for so long, the energy facilities are now too risky. Saddam could just blow them up so the U.S. doesn't get them."

"Why not a grain storage warehouse on the south side or something similar?" asked Harry.

"The military has been in and out of grain storage, moving food every day for the last month, because they're potential targets."

"How long do we sit?" asked Andre.

"Four days tops before the capture of the airport."

Bain laid out another map, this one of the airport. "This is the administration building."

Bain looked at the doubt on everyone's faces except Harry's. "You think it's risky because the airport has no cover. But that's why there won't be any military there, and the U.S. won't bomb it because they need it."

Irish cracked a smile.

Bain continued. "Ok. Second on the agenda...." He threw copies of two photos to the table. "I have received some new surveillance toys. It seems that when these guys went anywhere, a car always followed and looked out for a tail, making it hard to find out where these guys are making rounds. It's getting late in the game, and I want to at least know when these guys are on the move. We got locations on their two top guys, who are sitting tight. I want Tino and Andre on the Captain and Patrick and John on the Lieutenant. Harry will scope the route. Remember, if you can see them, they can see you, so use your heads."

CHAPTER
TWENTY FIVE

"Iraq has made efforts to cooperate, but still has to account for missing weapons."
Hans Blix's second report to the United Nations

Irish sat at a café with a newspaper and open laptop, occasionally looking over the rims of his sunglasses to the distant fourth-floor window of a six-story building at the end of a tee-bone intersection and the image of the same building on the computer screen coming through a mini-camera disguised as a pen in one hand. He grabbed John's attention before he completely walked past Irish, who had his chair up against the building. "Over here."

"Hey," John said, taking a seat.

"Got to keep your back to the wall on this one."

"Yeah right."

"It's hard to work the camera and the zoom at the same time. Especially with my shaky hands." Irish held his hands out, exposing, but jokingly trying to play down what has been months of alcohol abuse.
John faked a polite chuckle as he grabbed the pen camera.

"See the building at the end of the street? Point it in that direction and we'll work it up. Ok."

John looked to the building down the street and back again. "Ok. Yeah sure."

"Hold the pen with two hands and lean your head into your hands for stability. Look down to the paper like you're reading. Ok, Got the corner. Up slowly. Stop. Now over to your right slowly."
John struggled with his concentrated reading posture, just moving his hands.

"Stop," commanded Irish. "Wow, this is a pain."

"At least you don't have to pose."

"Shush. When you talk, the camera moves."

"Dick."
After ten minutes the Lieutenant walked past the window.

"Jackpot." exclaimed Irish, shutting the computer. "You can stop reading now."

"Seen enough?"

"Enough for now. You are lucky he wasn't sleeping."

"Who sleeps here?"

"True." Irish took a long drag from the hookah stem while John worked his neck side to side, taking out the kinks.
John's eyes landed on the tan car with smashed headlights. "What happened to your car?"

"Someone backed up into it parking." Irish quickly changed the subject. "Hey. You were late. You're never late."

"Fighting with Sue."

"In the romance capital of the mid-east? How? I don't believe it."

"Such a dick."
Irish raised his coffee in mock toast.

"Sue's been giving me the ice-queen treatment at work, and rightly so. She wants me to be around more to lean on and I haven't. Today was a continuation of the restaurant incident the other day."

"Oh boy. What did you tell her?"

"That I like to deal with things by myself."

"Which sounds like bullshit."

"Everything sounds like bullshit after you and Harry were seen several times in the middle of the day, in the middle of the work-week, lounging back, smoking and sipping coffee."

"Shit. What did you say?"

"I said you guys didn't work conventional hours."

"Even though the months before we were? You could have said that we were waiting around to see if our contracts are being renewed. You suck at this."

"She never told me what date she saw you. And you know, I'm glad I suck at this. I don't ever want to do this shit again."

"That's why Bain had a pimp's number for us. Not only did you commit everyday taboo by fucking your boss, you did it on a mission."

Both men sat, silence between them. The traffic signal on the corner cycled twice before John spoke. "I'm sorry Irish."

"*Sigh*…. No, I'm sorry. I've been working with sweaty Filipino and Russian grunts the whole time and I'm giving you shit. You were the only one working with a woman and a good one at that. Any one of us would have fallen in love. Harry and I are just as responsible for any *would-be* security breach, being friends with her and going out with the both of you."

A slight smile and nod from John concurred a friendship never damaged, even by the lecture just received. John took a drag from Irish's hookah stem.

"This shit is dragging out. If this goes on any longer, these people are going to turn on us."

"You just figured that out? These people have been spitting in our coffee for months." Irish laughed and took a sip, but the smile was brief. "I don't like to go out in my neighborhood at night."

"I'm talking about the people Bain deals with. If the French have more money or worse, influence at their embassy, they can buy off our connections with trips out of here for them and their families."

Irish was surprised he didn't see it coming himself. *Was it the alcohol?* He looked out to the street, letting the harsh revelation sink in. "Shit."

CHAPTER
TWENTY SIX

February 15, 2003

War protests again held worldwide, the largest being in Madrid, Rome, London and New York, each with an attendance estimated at 500,000.

In New York the protest route is fenced in along the curb and lined with police on the sidewalk. Entrance in and out of the protest route is legally available only at intersections. With still arriving protesters, the response of the police is to prohibit those who exit from the march for food or bathroom facilities any reentry.

Baton thrusting police and mounted units using their horses push back would-be participants and those meaning to re-enter away and out of sight of those in the march and the media. Protesters caught between the intersection and the sidewalk fence are arrested for loitering and/or blocking pedestrian traffic.

Daybreak

John was shocked upon finishing the climb up the stairs to see Sue at his door early, after finishing an all-nighter out with Irish and Harry. "Hey. This is a surprise."

"Hi."

John stood still.

"You going to let me in?"

"Yeah sure," he said, as if snapping to. He unlocked the door and walked straight to the kitchen. "I don't have any foo…."

Sue cut him off quickly. "I got the phone call."

John stopped in his tracks. "Oh wow. So, when do we leave?"

"Tomorrow."

"Really?" said John, trying not to let the lump in his throat crack his answer.

"I just came from Anna's. She was crying. I was crying. It was a mess."

John leaned in to hug Sue, but it was not reciprocated. Sue heard John's nervous swallow and stepped back with tear filled eyes. "John. Plane leaves tomorrow morning at 10:30. Do you want me to pick you up?"

"No," he said, unable to keep eye contact. "I will say goodbye to some people and meet you there."

"John? Are you really coming to the airport?"

"Yeah. What is it?"

"Remember we were talking about childhood not too long ago?"

"Yeah?"

"The last letter I sent back home was to my cousin. A lot of it was the day-to-day chaos, but also how I met this wonderful guy."

"Ok."

"Coincidentally, I received a letter back this week. Out of curiosity, she looked you up on one of those high school graduation class websites."

John's face paled as Sue continued with tears rolling down her face. "I guess the CIA forgot to tell you Johnathan Nariz was an all-star soccer player that's two years older and I've seen you play soccer, John. You stink!"

"Sue."

Sue started to fully cry. "I've been mad at you for not being there for me. But I can't believe you were going to leave me at the airport. Holy shit!"

"Sue I'm sorry."

"Leave me at the airport? No! I'm sorry because deep down I knew all along. You're always out, always eating out. I know what you get paid. Your suspicious friends. I knew it."

"I'm not CIA."

"Then what the fuck are you?"

"A thief."

"A thief?"

Sue's sadness turned to anger. "So, you're waiting for the war to start in order to steal something?"

Sue's disgust with his decision making was all too painfully familiar.

"My God. The CIA would have been more honorable."

"Sue please."

"You and your buddies are going to steal while other people's lives ending."

John stammered for words. "It...."

"Do I have that right?"

"It wasn't supposed to be like this. Everything has spun out of control. There's nothing more I can say."

"No! No there's not." Sue wiped the tears from her eyes. "You thoughtless bastard! Did you ever think of the trouble I or Anna could have been in if you got caught?" Sue trembled with rage. "I was in love with you for months and never knew your name. Ah....shit."

John said nothing as Sue again wiped away her tears, regaining composure. She opened the door. "I take it you're staying."

"Yeah."

"One last thing." Sue looked at John with steely demeanor. "My cousin never looked you up. You just got bluffed. You better work on your game. This place just may be your coffin."

Sue closed the door behind her, leaving John frozen. He thought of the date. It was the second loss of a woman he loved in less than eighteen months.

CHAPTER
TWENTY SEVEN

Between March 1, and March 6, 2003, Iraq destroys nineteen conventional weapons in contradiction of Resolution 1441.

At John's apartment, there was a knock at the door. Not expecting anyone, he tip-toed to the door until hearing Irish's voice.

"Hello. It's the Iraqi lottery commission. I have a check for you."

Shaking his head with a grin, John let him in. "I was just on my way to meet you."

"Yeah, I tried to call, but the cell towers are up and down again this week. Change of plans. Harry's at the café with the laptop waiting for you. Bain wants me and Andre off the streets until showtime."

"For what?"

Irish paused with a smile. "For being too white."

"Yeah, it's true," agreed John with a chuckle.

Irish's laugh and good mood appeared to be skin-deep. John looked down to the duffel bag in Irish's hand. "You moving in?"

"I just replaced four slashed tires on my car."

"What? Kids in the neighborhood fucking with you?"

"Kids, adults, the elderly, gremlins. Who knows? I'm no good to anyone if I can't get up and go when shit goes down. So yeah, I'm moving in. I just don't want to be quarantined in my dump."

"Yeah sure. No problem. Given the scarcities, four tires must have cost an arm and a leg."

"It cost me a over priced used car, cause I couldn't find tires anywhere."

"Fuck. Oh well. Make yourself at home." John grabbed his keys and headed for the door. "No pubes on the toilet, you fucking animal," he shouted.

"I'm gonna piss all over it!"

.
.

John sat, joining Harry at the stakeout.

"I just got tuned in. I take it you'll work the pen."

"Yeah, it's a special talent. Did Irish tell you where?"

"Yes. Fourth floor, third window from the corner."

John got into position, holding the camera pen with two hands and leaned his head forward as a tired man would just to get through the newspaper. "Got the corner yet?"

"Little to the right. Little more....got it. Slowly up. You're veering left. Move right slowly. Up just a little more. Got it! Now to your right, slow....slow....stop! Sit tight. And zoom." Harry looked to John. "You're good. How often you do this?"

"Once a day, every other day. It all depends if the right table is free."

"How long do you sit for?"

196

"Not too long. The guy I think is claustrophobic. Always pacing back and forth."

Suddenly the man appeared on Harry's screen. "Speak of the devil."

"That him?"

"Oh, yes, that is him."

John put down the camera and leaned back, working the kinks out of his neck. "How's Tino doing this by himself?"

"He's probably not. I offered to go out with him after this, but he didn't want to. Probably off getting high."

"That's great. Just fucken great."

"You know we are supposed to have people doing this type of work for us."

"Yeah well, that pool of people is drying up along with our clout."

"I know. That's why I said it."

"Then I'm sure you know all this surveillance is bullshit."

Harry grinned. "What? That there is a chance they have been watching us the whole time. Like right now. That *is* very likely."

John gave a subtle look to the windows surrounding. "Maybe since the meeting at the café."

"Perhaps since the meeting. Yes. That is what I would have ordered done." Harry looked over to John, who gazed at his coffee. "Have you run this past your partner?"

"We've talked about it. He's a big boy. He's been around the block."

"Ah yes."

Sensing the implication, John looked over, but now it was Harry who just stared out to the street as if avoiding eye contact, but John knew better, that it was only Harry in deep thought. He paused a moment before continuing. "So, we're going through the motions?"

"Going through the motions."

"So, while I have been foolishly romantically involved, you've been reading a lot about archeology at the city library in books and on the computer."

Harry, who knew where the conversation was being directed, asked, "What do *you* know about the plates, John?"

"I only know they are the first exhibit in the east wing, three together in one frame, each about 5x16 inches in length, they have a text on them that says only God knows what and that it pissed you off seeing them as the target item." John turned his chair to face Harry. "What happened to your poker face?" John asked with a smirk. "You showed your cards old-timer. You slipping?"

Harry rolled his eyes and looked back with a slight smile then ahead. "That argument we had at Christmas-time. I told you and Irish that we were stealing culture. And I knew better of it because, what is ancient culture, but a reflection of the economy. And economy, no more than a by-product of the richness of the terrain, what it has to offer of value for trade. Taking small objects from the casket of a working-class peasant would be stealing culture. This is bigger than that. This is *stealing history*."
John continued to silently listen on.

"Cuneiform text is the oldest written language that people have been aware of. It was the writing of ancient Sumner going back as far as 7000 years BC.
Most of the world has believed that there was no written civilization before that and some that it is when God created the world. These plates are of an earlier

unknown script, carbon-dated to roughly 15000 years BC."

"So, it fucks up the conventional time-line we've all been spoon-fed. Maybe it fucks with religion. What else?"

"What else? You ask that as if that is not enough to disturb the powers that be, both religious and political."

"Ok. So, what do the so-called *keepers of the keys* think it says?"

"I can't tell you what the keepers of the keys say, but there are a lot of people saying many of things. Varies on whose article you read. Could be outrageous or plausible, depending whether it is your propensity to look for answers in the stars rather than have the church tell you."

"Where are you going with this?"

"Did you notice that the first and second plates had what looked like lines and dots?"

"Yeah."

"Well, the first picture some say is the constellation where...." Harry held up his hands in quotations. "....the *builders* came from. A location of our angelic origins."

"None of this is new. People have been speculating forever who erected the pyramids, because no one can agree to a official story. And the old *we came from space* theory. The Scientologists have them beat already."

"Yes. Well, they are not new ideas, but neither has been backed up by intellectuals and carbon dating."

"And the second picture? If that is what it is."
Again, Harry held up quotations. "Some are saying, *"a place of eternal fire,"* others saying a location of a *"sky-fire-chariot"* landing site."

"Oh, you got to be kidding me. Why not say it's a energy vortex or a time porthole or something equally ridiculous," guffed John, as Harry patently waited to continue.

"I'm relaying to you all the speculation that I have read, both orthodox and the fringe."

"I have this distinct feeling you have decided to lead with the fringe."

Harry smirked and continued, "Maybe it's the next Rosetta Stone location, a scroll, a library, or temple." Harry shrugged his shoulders. "Could be treasure or just the next broken jar of dust." He then cracked a smile, "Only found provided they can dig up the other reference points on the plate."

"Which could be another 500 years from now or never."

"Perhaps."

"I don't fucken believe people are dying for this shit."

"Never know, John. It could be the location of the newest finite resource to be exploited."

"Is that also being said?"

"Of course. That's what's being said the most about...." Harry held up his hands with the gesture of quotations, "....the *eternal fire*."

"That at least would make more sense. But why are we stealing this thing again? I'm sure many already have the photo."

"It's not good enough to just have a photo. The writing is textured at points between the characters like fine braille. It has to be studied with magnification."

"You got to be fucken kidding me. Oh, and let me guess, the fella that made these assumptions is now at the bottom of the River Thames."

"No. Actually, a gas explosion at his house right here in Baghdad. The University of Baghdad had a arrangement with Oxford and was putting him up in a house."

"A *house*. Mmmm. Guy thought he had it made. I'll guess again. A house in Bain's neighborhood."

"Yep."

John turned to the street and leaned back, letting the information sink in. "What the fuck?" he grumbled.

A few cars passed beeping with passengers leaning out windows, waving Iraqi flags. Some on the sidewalk returned with a cheer.

"Did I miss something?" asked John.

"That weapons inspector from the U.N. said that Iraq is not a threat."

"Mmmm," replied John, with a roll of the eyes.

"Sad how a people will celebrate their country's impotence when the U.S. is breathing down their necks."

"I don't know what breaks my heart more, that or their romantic optimism."

"What do you remember about World War II, Johnny?"

"I wasn't there, *Abuelo*."

"Puta! In school. In school."

John laughed at seeing Harry get a little frustrated with the dumb answer punctuated by the Spanish word for *Grandpa*. He loved how Harry was still too cool to crack and get mad. "I didn't take school seriously, Harry. That's why I'm here. So you tell me instead."

"Psychological warfare is what Germany did to France and its neighbors. It's creating the belief that confrontation is avoidable if your country acquiesces to this term or that term. It is smooth politics -and strong bought-off media combined- to trick a populace to blame its own politicians who warned of war and advocated for a stronger defense against attack, should war happen. To paint a picture that there was *an out* and that their own politicians didn't take it."

"So, that's how Hitler marched into some of those countries with little fight?"

"Many of those nations were weary from the First World War. Especially France, who it is estimated to have lost one and a half million soldiers."

"Is that what you think Saddam is doing? What about all the antiaircraft guns I'm seeing placed around town?"

"I didn't say the psychological would work on him. He is czar here. Too powerful within his country to bow to political pressure. No one is getting elected to take his place. But remember, when social or economic conditions permit, there is another half to psychological warfare that's even more powerful than the citizenry believing there is a way out."

"And what's that?"

"Belief that an occupying force will bring a better way of life. It usually never does."

"Jesus Christ." John shook his head. "Ok. But what of the guns?"

"That's all for show. He knows he doesn't stand a chance. There has been a weapons embargo for years. So, despite what illegal arms buying avenues he has taken over the years, his military has a very finite supply that may be depleted after the first night of bombing."

"So, how do you think this whole thing plays out?"

"He will put on a futile military display, sacrificing all those that remain at their assigned cannons, during which time he will destroy all conscription records, allowing -when the time is right- his army to melt back into civilian life, where only some -due to the physiological warfare- will wage a guerrilla war in the urban centers to make city occupation very difficult."

"Smart strategy."

"That is the sum of the strategy in most countries when threatened by a larger, stronger army. The rest of the strategy is for a rebellion to get to the mountains or jungles and link strategic points between cities. Yet here it is only inevitable defeat, since there is no chance of taking the resistance outside the cities because of flat, open terrain. What resistance exists will be trapped in the cities, where the American forces will cordon off neighborhoods and go block by block and house by house."

John sat absorbing all that was said for a moment.
Harry shook his head. "It's almost a year ago when we were on that balcony in Asunción. Those were fun nights."

"A fucken year," replied John, shaking his head in disbelief. "Nights of drinking and dancing on the payroll. You knew it was all downhill from there." John looked over. "Harry. Was that the last time you...." Asking delicately, John let the *you* hang for a moment.
Harry rolled his eyes, "Got a piece of ass? Don't remind me."

A whistle blew and John and Harry turned to see a crossing guard holding up his hand, stopping traffic to let about thirty grade school students cross the street.
Upon seeing the children, Harry brought up the sensitive subject weighing on them both- as to whether Irish would compromise the mission. "Our boy is *not* doing well."

"Is anybody doing well? Have you slept? I haven't."
Harry looked back to the last few children crossing the street. "No. I haven't. But at least we are sober and not on the edge of tears every time we see children."

"Well, then, maybe there's something wrong with us. Did you think of that?"

"I'm just…."

John quickly stood up and threw a few dinars to the table. "Look! He moved in with me today. He's my problem. I'll take care of it. Call me tomorrow." John stormed off, leaving Harry at the table.

"Shit," Harry sighed, shutting the laptop and leaning back.

CHAPTER
TWENTY EIGHT

Arriving daily on the border, C-5s drop off US soldiers and military vehicles in preparation for a ground assault.

US ships moved on the high seas to join those ported in Kuwait City or the many more narrowly within international waters 15 miles off the Faw Peninsula, at the mouth of the Arvend Rud, just south of the marine city that bears its name.

.
.
.

WOOOSHHHHH.... At the last moment, Han Solo thrusted the Millennial Falcon into hyperspace, successfully avoiding capture by the Empire.
John, with a beer in each hand and a bag of chips under his arm, joined Irish at the couch. He looked from the poorly dubbed in Arabic, sci-fi classic to Irish, who sat fixated. Han and his rebel crew had just gotten caught in the tractor beam of the Death Star. "I take it you don't need a translator?"

"Fuck no." said Irish. "I've seen this a million times."

"You love this shit."

Nodding with a straight face, "I love this shit."

"Did you ever think you would be in the Middle East, hold up in an apartment, watching this?"

"Maybe. Always felt I was destined for greatness."

"Drinking Indian beer from a East German refrigerator, munching on Turkish potato chips and watching what is probably a North Korean TV. Who is better than you?"

"You're right Johnny." Irish took a long swig. "Why is the TV black and white?

"I got it at the outdoor market. I wasn't going to drag it back. Can't have everything you spoiled bitch."

"Ok, I got a question."

"Yeah?"

"How come every time you see a movie or TV show set in the future, whether it be Star Trek, Star Wars, Blade Runner or Fifth Element, they always show a city with flying cars sometimes even in bustling traffic?

"Cause the future is going to be anxiety filled and suck too? I don't know."

"If robots are doing all the heavy work and the menial tasks, where does anyone have to be? Where is there for people to go? You see that robot that Honda is working on?"

"Asimo."

"Yeah, that's it. It now walks with a swagger. What will it be capable of doing in a decade? Where is it all going. What are people going to do?"
John, knowing that Irish had been drinking and was now not so subtlety stressing the future his daughters were to inherit, tried to lighten the conversation. "Stay home and masturbate to the hottest robot porn."

"You're an ass."

KNOCK KNOCK KNOCK

"Who the fuck is that?" Whispered Irish, sitting up from the sofa.

"Food delivery!"

John smiled, got up and shut the TV. As he walked to the door he looked over his shoulder to Irish and whispered, "Obviously all that laser gunfire gets you jittery."

"Fuck you."

"Hey, hello." John opened up to Gabir who walked past him and right to the kitchen table with a heaping plate of lamb and rice.

"Malik got called away for a meeting before dinner. I hope you both are hungry."

"I am hungry, but wow that's a lot of food."

"It is not all for you, young man. Some utensils we need. Hello Mr. Irish."

Irish sat up and worked the kink out of his neck "Evening, Gabir."

John smiled to himself, knowing the real reason for the visit. He fired up the tea pot and brought cups, plates, and forks to the table. "To much estrogen in the apartment today?"

"What?"

"The girls driving you mad?"

"Oh. Yes. Today the two young ones are acting up with each-other," said Gabir, with his mouth full.

"Over telephone?"

"Same. Usually telephone or clothes."

"Well, Gabir you can seek refuge here anytime."

"I thank you."

The three men had already dug in, when the kettle whistled.

"I got it." John then poured each cup and rejoined the meal. "How's the baby?"

"Oh, she's good. Too little not to be. All kids are good until they lean to complain."

"Hey, Gabir. Have you noticed that John hums when he really enjoys the food?"

"I call bullshit," said John with a smirk.

"I call reality. It's true. Please Gabir, pass along the complements to you daughters, even if it's not in any known language."

Gabir laughed. "Maybe if I feed him more he will make a symphony." He then reached across the table with the serving spoon to add to John's plate, knocking over a tea cup. "Oh, my fault."

Irish looked around. "Where are the paper towels,"

"Shit. I'm out."

"Ok I'll use this." Irish, then threw down the days newspaper to soak up the spill and John re-filled the cup.

Both young men thought nothing of it and again it was back to the food.

Only Gabir leaned back, looking to the front page as it changed color with the absorption. "They are at the river again. At our gates. At Faw." Gabir's eyes still lingered on the headline.

The young men snuck a glance to each-other. John leaned in, looking to the paper, then to Gabir. "It appears so."

"I almost died there in 1986. The residents of Faw are tough people, not strangers to the conflict and destruction of war. They, more than anyone, know the risks of being strategically important yet vulnerable. My unit was supposed to go there in 1986, but due to an Iranian invasion of the city that cut us off from the garrison, we were unable. The city was captured by Iranian troops who overwhelmed soldiers who were then trapped behind enemy lines in the city. They were defeated block by block. It was a slaughter."

"What happened after that?" asked Irish.

Iran held the city for two years until expelled by us in a three-day massive ground and air-offensive, which resulted in the shelling of many of our own roads and buildings, a school and hospital included. We bullet holed and cratered the whole cityscape, killing many of our own citizens." Gabir paused, then asked, "Do either of you believe in fate?"

Both men shrugged their shoulders

"Neither do I know. I am here because either my unit was too late, or the Iranians were too early taking the city. All the experiences I have had in the last 17 years sometime seem by chance. An hour here, a minute or second there, all the difference in the world."

Irish asked, So, what of the city after?"
John wished he didn't ask, for he knew the answer.

"In the Gulf War, British and U.S. forces shelled what military installations we rebuilt at Faw. The naval blockade that followed shut the Tigris and Euphrates rivers off from all international shipping.
Irish processed the information and then inquired, "Ok. But so how did the people there support themselves? Or were they expelled by the Americans?"
"No. They were not expelled. Some of the citizens there, were permitted limited commercial fishing for sustenance or business."
"Oh, so nice of them," said Irish, looking at John, who ignored the obvious dig.
Gabir continued, "But how it was decided by the Americans, as to who would receive the fishing permits is still in the courts, with some pointing fingers, crying collaboration and traitor and others serving prison sentences."

As John and Irish sat silently for a moment. Gabir reached for the young men's empty plates and utensils, stacked them and pushed himself from the table. "As for Faw, so too, must the country endure whatever there is to happen

"Gabir, I was going to get that."

"I insist," he said, laying the plates in the sink and walking to the door with the dish and spoon he arrived with. "It is late and I'm sure the sisters are done fighting by now."

John nodded with a faint smile. "Yes. Let's hope so."

All then bid goodnight.

A moment passed. Irish leaned back in his chair, staring at the celling. "John."

"Yeah," said John, still sitting and looking blankly to the table.

"Gabir can't come here after 7p.m. if these are the fucking bedtime stories he's gonna tell."

"Agreed."

.
.

Unlike the residents of Faw, some of the crew and their rivals cannot draw purpose or strength from family or community, avoiding physical or mental deterioration.

Ex-pec-ta-tion:
Different from its dictionary synonym *anticipation*, is hinged on belief rather than hope. Negative expectation. or simply believing the worst to be inevitable, brings about anxiety that, if unchecked, eats at one's nerves with an insatiable appetite.

It's of great sadness, but no surprise to John, knowing that he'd find Irish drinking in a church pew after finding a simple *"went out"* note upon arriving home. Neither is it shocking to Louis, who peeked through the cracked bathroom door, to see Remy, tightening the tourniquet in an effort to find the vein.

Days for Bain, spent locked in the house with a bottle at his side, waiting for the phone to ring.

Nights for Andre and Tino, immersed in Baghdad's drug culture of smoking hash and drinking.

Harry, who has kept himself together through the year, froze upon hearing the loud horn at an intersection before stepping onto the crosswalk. He looked up to the remaining duration on the walk signal then to a traffic cop suspending the normal routine, allowing a convoy of military vehicles towing anti-aircraft guns to cross. Pensively, he looked on at the inevitable rapidly approaching.

CHAPTER
TWENTY NINE

Windows moved across the computer screen unbeknownst to the building's working-class residents. "Do I got it yet?" asked John, in his awkward camera holding posture.

"Stop. Right there, you got it." Harry steadied his chair, moving it closer to the table and reaching for the coffee cup. "Let's see how our boy is doing."
On the computer screen, nothing moved for six minutes until a woman rushed past the window. Harry sat back and looked down the street to the building. "John. Go back to the bottom corner and start again slowly. I got the wrong window."

"Ugh! You fucken serious?"

"Shut up. Back slowly. Down, down. Ok, stop. Up slow one... two... three... four... Stop. Over slow one...two...got it."
On the screen a minute passed before the same woman passed the window again. A young boy of five looked out the window and then was pulled back by his mom.

"Shit," Harry exclaimed. He patted John on the back. "Heads up man."

"What happened?"
Harry shut the laptop. "They're on the move."
Both men rose from the table.

"Are you sure?"

"We checked it twice. Call Tino to see what happened to his mark."

"Can't get a signal. You try."

Both men jumped in the car.

"No good," said Harry.

John tried again. "This shit's gotten worse. What the fuck!"

"There's a war coming. Could be cell traffic or the military is switching the signals over for themselves."

"Call Andre."

Harry broke through to Andre, but it was all interference. "Andre! Where's Bain? Shit! I got static. Where's Bain? Ok, meet you there." Harry snapped the phone shut.

"What's going on?"

"Drive north. We're going to meet up. I'll keep trying Irish."

.

Irish, while on the phone with Harry, checked his pistol and clips, stuffed it into his waistband, then started to pack his duffel bag. "Ok see you there in a little while." CLICK "This is bullshit!" he muttered to himself.

KNOCK KNOCK KNOCK

Irish in quick reaction pulled the gun, leveling it to the door. Keeping an eye on the door, he walked slowly to the window overlooking the front of the building. He peered through the mesh curtains without movement on the right side of the window. Nothing unusual about the street and sidewalk, no strange cars or suspicious men to be seen.

KNOCK KNOCK KNOCK

Irish positioned himself, aiming from behind the wall separating the kitchen from the living room area.

Between the knocking, a familiar voice, "Irish! I heard you inside. Open up!"

Irish immediately lowered his arm and took a deep breath. "Shit." He pulled open the door. "Sue. What the fuck…."

"Save any bullshit. I know what you guys are up to," said Sue, as she stormed past Irish into the apartment. "Where's John?"

"What the fuck are you doing here? You've got to get out of the country."

"I'm not going anywhere. Where's John?"

"Sue. The money for my family is in your name. You have to go home!" declared Irish, with eyes wide and voice stressed.

"Why would you do that? How did you get my information?"

Irish stood, mouth open, with no words.

With a look of disgust, she shook her head. "Oh my God. Never mind. I don't want to fucking know. "Where's John?"

"Not here. I'm on my way to meet him and Harry. Go home. I will have him…."

"I'm coming with you."

"No, you're not."

"Are you really going to leave me here? You didn't just recently pull out that gun for nothing."

Irish looked to his waist, where his shirt only half covered the pistol due to quick hasty placement. "Shit."

⋮

John and Harry arrived at the café. Five customers sat at tables out front and seven more at the

214

window on the inside. To the left a man stood behind a small counter with a register, coffee maker and a soda fountain. Toward the back before the kitchen, Bain, Andre and Tino sat at three tables joined together. To the right on the opposite wall, a 4-year-old daughter of a customer sat playing with two small dolls alone at a table.

Harry and John approached the crew. Irish entered, gestured to John and pulled him to the side.

"Sue's back."

"What?" exclaimed John, barely keeping the surprise under his breath.

"She showed up right before I was leaving. She wouldn't stay put. She's waiting in the car."

Both looked over to Bain and the crew seated at the table, then to Sue walking to the front door.

"*Was* in the car."

"Shit," John said under his breath.

John and Sue's eyes briefly locked as she walked past him, taking a chair at the table next to the little girl in the back on the opposite side. They exchanged smiles.

Irish joined the crew at the table. Only John remained standing.

Bain let out a sigh with his head still in the newspaper. "I told you guys how I felt about more than two of us in public at the same time. But hey." Bain looked up directly to Sue, raising his tone of sarcasm with each word. "It's nice to see John's old boss has decided to join us." Sue returned with an icy stare. His head dropped back to the newspaper.

The five men scanned the room, out the window and one another.

Bain continued. "There was a suspicious vehicle on my block when I did my drive-by. I got some people checking it out. So, we all had an interesting day."

215

John, still for a moment, looked Bain up and down. "Did the French call you?"

"You guys would have been told if they did," Bain replied, with a mock tired tone.

Irish looked to John and with a motion of the head, gestured to Bain. "Tell him."

Bain looked up to John. "Tell me what?"

"I think the French are going to buy allegiance through offering trips out of here with the help of the embassy."

"That's it?" he scoffed "You don't think I thought of that?"

"Is it true?" asked Andre and Tino in united alarm.

"How am I supposed to know? I can't make a call half the time and the people I want to talk to can't answer the other half."

Tino and Andre were visibly shocked by Bain's lack of control and leadership for the first time.

The man behind the register raised the volume on the TV and all the men turned upon hearing President Bush giving Saddam forty-eight hours to leave the country.

Bain looked up with a smirk. "Well, there you have it. Almost time." Again he returned his attention back to his paper.

Harry scanned the room, the customers, the man at the register.

"Almost what?" asked John. "Time to die?"

Bain looked up.

"It's fucken over."

"Over? Who the fuck are you? What are you doing here anyway, with your sorry guilt? Were you bribed to be here? Because if you were, I don't fucking need you. You're just a liability."

216

The workers and the customers watched as the argument unfolded. The little girl stared in confusion at Bain. Sue pulled her chair next to her's, and in Arabic quietly asked, "Tell me what you're playing."

"I'm a liability? We're out-manned and obviously out-funded. Look at us! Six sitting ducks."

Bain stood. "You ignorant dipshit. Do you know how many times this has been done? There's always guys to make a grab in crises, natural or man-made, Hurricane Andrew, the Blitzkrieg, Leningrad, Berlin. Maybe as far back to the fall of fucking Troy and…!" Bain trailed off the rant as he realized John's eyes were elsewhere.
"Look back to the TV Bain."
Bain looked to the screen, showing the museum's art being taken down to a basement for protection."
"Do we have a man on the inside or are we really going to dig all night for this shit.? Oh wait, that was rhetorical. We don't have anybody in our pocket anymore. We don't even know if that basement is the museum's or somewhere else completely."
Bain turned around with fury. "Fuck you, you little shit!"
"It's over Bain! Whatever deal your employer had with some rogue British or American spooks to create the element of surprise didn't work." John said the next slow and pronounced and obnoxious. *"It's fucken over."*
"It's called work, you cowardly piece of shit. Things happen but you make the job work!"
John was silent as he stared at the madman.
"I made my bones getting Noriega's gold. I'm not going to lose…."
Andre interrupted. "Hey, boss. I think that guy has a signal," he said, pointing to a man outside on his cell phone. Bain looked over, then back to John with

contempt. He opened his cell, walking to the front entrance as John took a seat with the men. Harry and Irish, the only ones to give him a look and nod of approval.

Irish stood and gestured to Harry and John to follow suit. Tino and Andre stayed seated looking on as the three men rose. Irish then leaned over the table, hand on the gun in his waist. "The four of us are leaving this place. *Fuck you* if you try to stop us."

As Bain walked to the door, a car rolled up slowly. Out of the vehicle windows, men quickly postured to shoot. The front windows shatter as the customers outside, Bain and the customers inside close to the windows were riddled with bullets.

The crew flipped the table over. Sue grabbed the young girl and hit the floor.

Tino rose from behind the table with a Glock, returning fire and took a bullet to the neck.

The man behind the register came up from behind the counter with an AK-47 and was hit twice in the chest.

Outside four gunmen got out of the car. Two ran down the alley to the rear entrance of the café, leaving two to cover the front.

The little girl screamed, confused and frightened by the sounds of chaos and deafening gunfire.

Andre crawled along the floor to retrieve the counterman's gun and ran off to the kitchen with Harry following behind.

Inside the café, John and Irish tipped over three tables together for cover. John with Tino's Glock and Irish with his own, fired blindly from behind the tables.

Behind the café the two gunmen were counting out the rear entrance doors from the corner.

Andre kicked open the back door, exiting to the alley firing, downing the other two gunmen as they reached for the door handle. Andre, still in motion, fired a finishing burst of rounds at each man as they lay on the concrete. Harry grabbed a machine gun from one of the fallen men and followed Andre down the alley toward the street.

John's Glock now empty, "You got to cover me."
Irish peeked between the two tables. "Ok. Go!"
Irish commenced fire as John grabbed a table by the trunk and used it as a shield, making his way to Sue and the young girl.
John and Sue crouched tightly around the young girl behind the table.

Andre and Harry reached the mouth of the alley. Andre took cover at the corner of the building and engaged the two gunmen in front, killing one as he turned upon hearing the shots

Harry provided cover, allowing Andre to work his way closer from car to car toward the storefront, engaging the last assassin, a man in his early twenties who was no match for the two combat veterans. The youth scurried across the street, narrowly being missed, as bullets hit the pavement around him.

Harry postured and waited for a clean shot, as the last surviving gunman kept his head down and moved behind parked cars. Once reaching the corner, he ran for it, just as Harry had anticipated. The young man crashed to the street after taking two bullets through his back. Harry, who hadn't killed since Angola, lowered the gun, gazing at the lifeless man lying on his chest. He closed his eyes and dropped his head, taking a deep breath, unhappy with the action he has taken and the situation he allowed himself to be a part of. But at the core he is a soldier and knows this is not the time for reflection.

With the shooting over, Irish peeked over the table. "Holy shit."
John, Irish and Sue slowly rose from behind the tables. Hearing a choking and gurgling behind Irish, John rushed to Tino's aid, who, still conscious, clutched his bleeding neck.

Irish and Sue, now holding the little girl, stood quietly looking at the carnage throughout the room.
Sue embraced the crying child in her arms, keeping her back to the site surrounding them.
        "Where's my daddy?"
        "He's went to get help," she responded softly in Arabic. Sue's eyes darted across the floor at all the bodies around the room that could be the girl's father. "Shit."

A young uniformed Baghdad street-cop rushed into the café shouting and nervously pointing his gun at Irish. John listened from behind the table, where he struggled to save Tino's life. "Shit."

Irish winced with pain as he laid the gun on the floor, but the policeman was still yelling. Slowly raising his hands, he called to John. "Hey, mate. You want to talk to this guy?"

"I'm not armed! I'm not armed!" John said in Arabic, slowly raising his hands from behind the table and then standing. "Officer, please listen to…."

"Shut your face!" the officer yelled back in Arabic, pointing the gun back and forth between Irish and John.

Sue stood frozen, holding the child, who again started to cry, listening to the exchange. "Oh my God. Oh my God," Sue whispered to herself.

The police officer clicked the radio microphone clipped to his shirt. "Command, come in." A voice response returned over the receiver.

John and Irish flinched as two shots rang out in the café, one to the body and other to the head, dropping the young officer. Andre, lowering his gun, entered through the front window with Harry, walking through the bodies and broken glass. John shook his head at Andre and returned to Tino's aid.

"You had to kill him?" yelled Irish.

Andre paid no mind to the question slash comment. "Can you please shut that kid up." He took a long look at Bain, who laid dead, face up, with eyes open. He then looked around the floor. "We got to find Bain's cell phone!"

Harry walked around kicking debris.

Irish shook his head, staring at the dead policeman. "We fucked up big time."

"Hey! You two listening?"

John, with his finger in Tino's neck, jumped back as Andre shot Tino three times in the chest. John sat wide eyed on the floor with his back to the table, hands covered in blood. Irish stared at Tino, holding his hands on top of his head as if trying to keep it together.

Andre unemotionally took all his ex-partner's identification and cell phone and reiterated. "We need that phone! We need those numbers!"

Harry held up Bain's cell phone. "Got it."

"Ok, let's go," bellowed Andre.

John approached Sue, who just re-comforted the child. She was gazing in the opposite direction. "Sue. Get to the hospital. They're going to need you there. Take the kid with you."

"Hey, John. The kid's a witness."

Harry and Irish immediately turned their guns on Andre.

"Don't even think about it," said Harry.

"You guys are going to shoot me?"

"I'm thinking about it," said Irish.

"I live close and haven't been to my place in weeks since the crackdown on foreigners," Andre said flatly.

Andre was still as Irish took from him the AK47. "Well, you can take the rest of the day off. You stupid fuck."

John turned back to Sue. "Sue, take the kid."

"I can't," she said, pausing to swallow the lump in her throat. "I'm in the movies."

John looked in the direction of Sue's stare to the surveillance camera on the wall. "Shit! Hey, we're on camera!"

Andre scanned the room, finding two more cameras. "Shit."

"Where's the recorder? Look for the recorder," yelled Harry.

Throughout the café were bookcases, shelves and cabinets filled with magazines, books, and trinkets. The crew scrambled, tearing the place apart in search of recording equipment.

Irish went through the kitchen shelves. He stopped upon seeing paper napkins, lifting his shirt and pulling his pants low, exposing the small wound to his abdomen, thinking it had to only be a piece of a bullet that had ricocheted off the floor. Irish, glad he wore black this day, stuffed the napkins against the hole, then shouted from the kitchen, "It could be anywhere. Maybe there's a basement."

Harry, standing on a chair to reach a shelf, looked out to the growing number of people that were gathering across the street. More than a few of the onlookers had their cell phones out.

Andre took notice of Harry's stare. "We gotta go!"

"Shit," exclaimed Irish, exiting the kitchen.

John again approached Sue, who had comforted the child since the shoot-out. The young girl was awake, yet in an exhausted daze, she rested her head on Sue's right shoulder. Sue, humming a soft lullaby, was still rocking her back and forth while rubbing her head and back. "Sue. We got to go."

A police siren wailing in the distance is heard by all.

Sue nodded and slowly put down the child and met her eyes. "Do you hear the police?"

"Yes," the girl meekly responded.

"I'm going to fix this for you."

Andre looked on, shaking his head and clenching his jaw as Sue gathered the young girl's toys, reset the table and seated her in the chair facing away from the bodies.

"Don't turn around. Stay here. The police will be here very soon."

The young girl nodded.

"Can we go now?" Andre grumbled.

Irish, staring at Andre, gestured with the pistol to the back door.

The young girl looked on as the crew and Sue headed for the back door. Sue looked back with tear filled eyes.

CHAPTER
THIRTY

Upon entering Andre's dark apartment, Irish pushed past Andre, urgently looking for the bathroom to repack the wound. Flipping the light switch, Andre looked to Harry and gestured to the bathroom door. "What the fuck is his problem?"

"He had to go," was Harry's dead-pan response as he walked past and laid the shot cell phone on the kitchen table along with a Swiss Army knife and an eyeglass screwdriver set.

Andre, John and Irish took chairs at the table. Sue started to drag a step stool to the corner of the room. John offered his chair in exchange. He tried to read her face but she moved the step stool around him, looking away and not acknowledging the gesture.

The apartment was no more than an old, basic, white painted, florescent-lit one bedroom with a small kitchen. On the poorly rough painted walls and cabinets were the trailing brown dots of roach defecation.

Six eyes looked to Harry, who remained standing, hands on the table, staring across at the toaster in thought. "Do you have an alarm clock?" he asked, quickly snapping to.

"Yeah. In the room."

Irish asked, "Does it even matter if we get a hold of someone? They'll probably tell us to just finish what we started."

"True," said Andre. "But if they want the job done and we need more firepower, they will have to come through."

In his peripheral vision, John caught Sue shaking her head.

Harry returned with an early 1980s General Electric alarm clock. The clock was non-digital, boasting a flip number display with a small motor inside that advanced time by rotating numbered panels on a rolodex type mechanism, a micro version of the schedule timetables seen at train terminals all over the world still.

All were quiet as Harry proceeded to take apart the alarm clock to retrieve the small gauge wires to the motor and smaller wires bridging circuit boards.

Sue leaned back in the chair, looking on from the other side of the kitchen and the men silently watched, occasionally each lending a third hand. Hours passed as at first Harry disassembled Bain's and his own cell phone -which were different- trying to use the clock motor wires with a removed board resistor to jump power from his cell battery, Bain's cell chip to Harry's screen, finally then in desperation stripping one of the small gauge wires and trying different combinations to bridge the circuitry over a broken board.

By daybreak-

"It's useless. We're not going to get any info from this phone," said Harry, frustrated, laying down the mini screwdriver and removing his glasses.

Andre stood, punching one of the metal cabinets. "Shit! Any ideas?"

Irish looked up from the floor. "Are there any embassies left?"

"They're all gone." Harry paused for a moment and continued as if speaking to himself. "That ship was maybe available at one time, but has since sailed."

"Kurdistan?" mentioned John, knowing that it had been a breakaway region since the inception of Iraq.

"We just can't drive out of town," indicated Harry.
Sue chimed in, "There has to be somewhere we could go to." The tone was more a question than statement.

"We will be treated as spies and tortured," answered Andre demonstrably, slouched in his chair, with head leaning over the back rest, looking at the ceiling as if the question was so stupid it sucked the life out of him.

"I didn't say going to the author...." Sue embarrassingly started to reply until Andre started to repeat himself.

"Enough!" Harry interrupted, as he stood, cutting of Andre's rant.
Andre shut his eyes as Sue continued. "....what if we went by where the new media is camped out? CNN, BBC, all the big names are there."
Andre slowly opened his eyes and looked to Harry with a smile. Since you feel I was picking on your friend's girlfrie..."
John straightened in his chair. "Fuck you Andre!"
Andre ignored John and continued while maintaining eye contact with Harry, "Like I said, since you feel I was picking on our nice doctor here, you tell her." He then gestured with his thumb to John. "You know *he* don't want to be the one."

Harry let out a sigh. "Sue, that area is blocked off. We could never get close enough without getting caught.

Even if noticed by the media, the military or police would still take us away *even* in front of the cameras. It's too late. We have gone too far. So, he *is* right. We would all be tortured to death. Including you. Even if the café cameras were just for show and no tape exists, there is a dead police officer and people outside the café witnessed a Asian woman leaving with armed men."

John turned and briefly met Sue's eyes and looked back to the table. Harry sat back down.

"Do you think our getaway ambulance is staked out?" asked Irish.

"Do you want to take the chance?" Andre replied.

John leaned in, placing both hands on the table. "Ok. We got to pool our money. Harry. How much have you saved?"

"I got about twenty."

"Andre?"

"Nothing. I had too good a time."

The apartment was an obvious flop-house building for the lonely, retired, broke or in Andre's case, for someone who pissed away money the minute they got it. Looking around at the conditions, no one thought to suspect Andre was holding out on money.

"What a fucking professional," said Sue, snarkily from the corner.

John looked over, annoyed. "Sue!"

"Is that your way of jabbing back at me, Doctor? I am more professional than a boss that falls for her criminal fake subordinate." Smiling, Andre continued, "The only one of us that came in broke and owing money, I might add."

Irish quickly reacted, "You dirty Slav piece of shit! You...."

"Irish!" John interrupted. "I got this." John stood. "Ok. Irish and I got money at my place. We'll go there, then pick up Harry's cash and see if we could work out something with one of the anti-Saddam clerics."

"Ok. Let me take a piss," said Irish, standing.

"That's number four," remarked John. "You ok?"

"What are you, my mother?" he shot back.

John looked to Harry, who just shrugged his shoulders. Sue finally spoke. "Everyone fill your water bottles."

On the way to the door, Andre reached for the AK-47 as Irish exited the bathroom. Quickly Irish leveled his gun to Andre's head.

"Relax partner," said John, holding the AK-47's magazine.

"Maybe tell me you have the ammo next time," said Irish, annoyed.

"Sorry partner."

Andre turned to Irish. "This is the second time you've pulled a gun on me."

"Next time I will just blow your stupid, low-life brains out," said Irish with a glare.

Andre didn't respond, instead he held out his hand to John.

"No. I will give it to you when we're outside."

Andre slung the gun over his shoulder and turned to the door.

"Wouldn't you rather take something smaller?" asked Harry.

"No."

"There are checkpoints everywhere," said John.

"Fuck it!" Andre snapped. "I'll drive separately."

"You're too white to drive separately," remarked Harry.

Andre walked to the door with no reply.

Harry shook his head. "Ok. Have it your way."

Andre walked to his car with John walking ten feet behind him, Irish's pistol at his side.

Andre opened his door and again held his hand open for the magazine.

"You know you were very right. I was in the negative when I showed up. Haven't been pillaging during war and acts of God like you all these years."

They now stood four feet apart, face-to-face.

"Are you sure that's true, John? You must have done something to get here?" He smiled. "Think really hard."

John didn't acknowledge the point. He would save the introspection of similarities for later. Instead he spoke without missing a beat. "I once robbed a bank. I didn't make a career choice out of it and I sure as fuck didn't pick the bones of my own people."

Andre said nothing.

John walked around Andre. "You wanted the big-boy gun. You got it." John smashed the butt of the pistol through the back-seat window. "Now you can bring up the rear and watch our tail," he said, throwing the magazine to the back seat of the car.

Andre stood seething, his jaw clenched, as John knocked clean from the window frame the remaining tempered glass with the gun.

John stepped back from the window with a smile. "There. That doesn't look too bad now, does it?"

Irish and Harry pulled alongside them.

John looked back to Andre. "You can feel free to take this up with me in Dubai after this is all over. But until then, please keep up your professionalism." John then handed off the pistol to Irish who sat passenger side and walked to his car, where Sue waited inside.

"Keep up, asshole," Irish said with a smile to Andre as he and Harry drove off.

Driving away, Irish looked in the rear-view mirror as Andre left the parking spot. "I know he can't accurately aim and shoot while driving, but did we really give this psycho sociopath behind us a AK-47 and purposely drive in front of him?"

"He doesn't speak the language and is in big trouble here without us. He needs us and he knows it. Problem is, we need crazy people who can fight."

"Strange alliances."

"Yes, they are."

"You a wise old fucker, ain't ya, Harry."

"Mmmm."

Harry again joined Irish's eyes in the rear-view mirror at the traffic light, then back to the road when it changed. "If he wanted to do it, he would have already. But keep an eye on him in the mirror anyway. You're right, he can't aim. But you can. If he raises that gun, put two through the windshield and one through the radiator."

The Baghdad morning commute had already begun. John and Sue led in the first car, Harry and Irish in the second, with Andre following up the rear. The three cars were staggered, but still in sight of one another as they weaved through the weekday rush.

In John's car, Sue sat passenger side. After a few minutes John broke the silence. "Now is a good time to have on your hijab and veil. You have it?"

"I always do," she said, reaching in her bag." Sue always kept a hijab and veil handy for trips into ultra-religious neighborhoods.

"You shouldn't have come."

"I know," she replied meekly, not wanting a fight. She hoped John would let it go for now.

"You said this place was going to be my coffin." Then he said, raising his voice, "Are you trying to lay in it with me?"

Sue coolly replied, "I said this place *might* be your coffin." But that was all Sue could say clearly before the crying. "I had no idea the shit you were dealing with. I wanted to get you out of this."

"Well, the boss is dead. I'm out of it now. Just a new set of problems. How the fuck were *you* going to get me out of this?"

Sue sobbed, hardly able to get the words out. "I wanted to tell you...."

"Tell me what? That this shit is wrong?"

"I wanted to tell you...."

"Knew it, know it and heard it from you once already!"

Screaming, Sue finished her sentence. "We're having a pill baby!"

In Harry's car, Irish leaned against the window, trying not to move. He straightened up to pull the flask from his jacket and took a swig.

Harry looked over. "You better take it easy. You don't look too good."

"It doesn't matter anymore," he said, fully aware of the tick-tock mortality of a gut wound and the grave situation of inability to seek help for it.

"What?"

"Nothing," Irish said, already feeling the pain and fever of the sepsis from digestive juices poisoning his bloodstream. He grabbed a pen sitting in Harry's cupholder, holding it within a fist and occasionally clicking the button.

Harry looked over. "Don't write your will yet."

Irish put the pen in his mouth, then removed it between his middle and fore-finger. Looking back to Harry with a smile, "This is just one of those times when I would like to have a cigarette." Turning back to the road ahead, "But hey, you never know."

In John's car, all was reflective silence until he noticed what held up traffic. "Shit."
Sue straightened up and looked in the mirror. "What is shit?"

"In front."
Sue peered ahead, seeing a checkpoint where cars were being stopped randomly.

"Oh no."

"Keep cool. Dead cop or not, there is not a lot of resources being devoted to sifting through a video with all this shit going on. Get your doctor ID out."
Harry and Irish looked ahead, as did Andre.

John and Sue arrived at the checkpoint only to be greeted by Asera's husband, Malik. John and Sue sat silently as Malik gave their car the visual once-over in front of another soldier.

"You two better be leaving," he whispered in Arabic.

"I got two behind, black and white guy, in one, white guy alone in another." whispered John.
Malik gave a subtle nod and they drove on.
John and Sue nodded and drove off, but not far due to the morning gridlock. Malik waved the next few cars through, including Harry's, upon seeing Irish passenger side. John, looking in the rearview mirror, saw Malik get a call on the radio and run to the command post on the side of the road. Another soldier took his place.

"Shit."

"What?" asked Sue, turning her head before being scolded by John.

"Don't turn around!"
Harry, Irish, John, and Sue were stopped in traffic, watching helplessly as Andre was waved over to the

side of the road. Andre kept still, but shifted the clutch to the reverse position with his right foot on the brake. A second command, this time in English, orders Andre to the side.

The soldier approached the vehicle from the front. Coming closer, he raised his gun and yelled for backup, upon recognizing the older army-issue AK-47 shoulder strap around Andre. The soldier came around to the driver's side as another took position at passenger side and one in front. All three men postured in combat position.

Again, Andre was ordered from the vehicle. Andre stalled in his car, hands up, but only shoulder high, with elbows at the side. Behind Andre, cars emptied out as the standoff unfolded.

"Don't do it," pleaded Harry, as if trying again to talk reason with Andre through telepathy.

"No no no," said John, gritting his teeth.

Andre floored it and quickly released the clutch. In a reverse drift, he raised his gun with futility, prompting the three soldiers of superior position to commence fire. Shot multiple times and with muscle tissue too torn to raise his hands, Andre's last action was squeezing the trigger below the dash.

Andre's muzzle flash was seen all the way from John's car.

"Ah fuck," John groaned.

Looking away from the rear-view mirror, Harry closed his eyes and dropped his head to the steering wheel.

Irish too, closed his eyes for a moment. "Shit."

More soldiers raced from the command post as the traffic started to move.

"Bastard," was Sue's only reaction, prompting John to look over.

From Sue's nurturing perspective, Andre was just a killer thug who would have killed the little girl in the café for being a witness.

For John and Irish, it was a matter of strength in numbers slowly diminishing.

As a military man, Harry who in the firefight, although brief, fought along Andre. To him it was the loss of a very unlikeable yet very capable asset, one who even, if only subjectively, saved their lives.

:

John, Irish, Sue and Harry entered John's apartment. John immediately rummaged through the cabinets and refrigerator, taking out food jars filled with cash.

Harry and Sue took seats at the kitchen counter.

Harry noticed Irish staring out the window. "Hey, man. Stay away from the windows."

Irish stood unresponsive as he looked below to a small group of children crossing the street on their way to school.

Harry looked to John, gesturing with his head to Irish.

John then walked up behind Irish. "Partner, we got money to get out of here, but we got to get moving."

"I got to take a shit," he replied, walking past both men and Sue -without eye contact- to the bathroom.

"Irish," Sue called with no acknowledgment.

Harry and John looked to each other puzzled by the behavior.

"John. Let him stay here and we'll get the cash from my place."

"No no no Harry. He's coming with."

"He needs to get his head together. I'll go and come back."

In the bathroom, Irish leaned on the sink vanity, then turned on the faucets.

"We hardly have phone service. We're not splitting up."

"Ok, but you better tell him to hurry up."

Sue walked around the counter and whispered, "I don't like the way he looks."

Harry gestured to the bathroom door.

John rolled his eyes. "Partner. We got to get rolling."

"Why don't you guys go and come back," Irish responded from behind the door.

"Our phones aren't dependable. We're not splitting up."

Irish placed the gun on the bathroom sink and looked into the bathroom mirror. He then opened his button and fly to repack the wound. When he removed the napkins, what little clot there was, came away with the packing, allowing the alcohol thinned blood to run down his legs, soaking his pants and dripping to the tile. He looked back to the pale reflection in the mirror.

Harry and John, both showing impatience, looked to each other with shared frustration. John then looked to Sue, who shrugged her shoulders.

Irish now sat on the toilet crying. His hands shook as he wrote a note on toilet paper.

Harry paced the floor. "He's been in there awhile."

Sue noticed droplets of blood on the floor and leaped to the bathroom door, trying to open it. "Irish!" she screamed hysterically, banging on the door.

John was taken back. "What the…."

"He's bleeding! Get it open!"

John kicked the door in. Irish looked up half dazed, still holding the pen. The floor of the bathroom and toilet were covered in blood.

John knelt down to check the wound. "Shit."

Harry looked over John's shoulder. "Dios mío."

Sue knelt next to John. "Why didn't you tell us?"

"Because I knew it was mortal," he said, both laughing and crying.

Irish handed John a half-written note. "My name is Daniel Sullivan. I have an ex and two girls, five and six in Cork. The…."

John put the note to the side. "I don't want to know this shit. Come on. We got to get you out of here."

"You gotta take the note. Please!"

"I'm not taking a goodbye note. I'm taking you."

"Sue! I sent the money info and ex's address to the address on your passport." He looked to Sue with a smile. "Sorry for being sneaky."

Sue reached for his hand. "It wasn't sneaky, it was smart."

John struggled to pick up Irish.

Harry looked on. "John. He lost a lot of blood."

"Harry please!"

Harry helped John drag Irish out into the hallway, where all the neighbors clamored due to the commotion. They stopped, both to re-grip Irish for the trek down to the street.

Irish locked eyes with a girl of about seven, then looked up to her parents and all the adults standing about. "You're all going to be bombed!" he yelled to the onlookers.

John and Harry didn't acknowledge it as they dragged Irish to the stairwell.

"It's going to happen in a couple of days," Irish continued to shout, gasping in between as they passed people who stood at each landing that had come out due to the commotion. "It will be worse than the first time…. *Gasp*…. They're going to take the city."

Sue ran back to the apartment to grab the cash, gun, and food. As she bagged everything, she could still hear Irish's dying man confession as John and Harry dragged him down the stairwell to the street. Leaving the apartment, she was confronted by Gabir.

"Sue. Is it true?"

Sue looked to Gabir in his doorway, then over his shoulder into his apartment, where his nieces looked on, waiting for an answer. Asera, the most anxious of the three, glared at Sue as she cradled the oblivious, happy five-month-old girl Sue held and fed two months earlier on New Year's Eve.

Irish, now dragging his feet had become almost dead weight. John and Harry struggled to get the car door open and place him carefully passenger side, as he still confessed, but now to the people on the street. "The U.S. is going to occupy Baghdad! The bombing starts in a couple of days!" His voice growing tired.

Sue came out from the building wiping away tears.

A crowed gathered around the car, looking at the spectacle.

After they set Irish in the passenger seat, John got behind the wheel. Harry and Sue jumped in back.

"John. The note. The money….get it to my family."

"Shush. We'll both get it to your family."

"You got to get to my apartment. I…." Irish shut his eyes.

"Partner? Irish!"

Harry reached over from the back seat, feeling for a pulse at the neck. "He's dead. Let's take my car."

"Oh Irish," Sue said softly, again welling up with tears. She fought back the crying, covering her mouth.

John stared at his lost friend as a siren grew louder in the background.

"Come on," said Harry, taking stock of the situation.

John grabbed Irish's keys and cell phone. Sue kissed her hand and touched it to Irish's cheek.

John, Sue and Harry got out of the car amid an angry crowd.

A man in his late twenties stepped forward. "How does he know these things?"

The three were unresponsive as they walked to Harry's car.

The young men of the crowd broke away and followed closely.

A voice called out from the group. "Did you kill him because he did not keep your secret?"

The men picked up pace and surrounded them.

Before things could get physical, Harry fired the pistol in the air, dispersing the crowd, sending men running and diving over parked cars.

The three jumped into the car. Harry took off with John passenger side and Sue in back.

The men quickly reassembled, throwing rocks and bottles at the fleeing car. John, Sue and Harry ducked, hearing two gunshots.

Blocks away, Harry rolled down the window. "Shit. Give me those cell phones."

John handed them over without question to watch Harry throw them and his out the window.

"What the fuck?"

"If the authorities got Andre's cell phone, they could get our signal."

Harry then threw the gun out the window.

"What's wrong with you?"

"Out of bullets."

"Oh, we are sorry."

CHAPTER
THIRTY ONE

"How much farther to your place?"

"It's the building at the end of the block. Third floor, blue shutters."

As they approached, Harry noticed one of the shutters cracked open. He drove past, mentioning nothing of it.

"What are you doing?" asked John.

"I always do a drive-by and park around the block."

Harry parallel parked the car. "Wait here. Keep an eye on the car."

"Hurry up."

John and Sue watched Harry as walked away.

"Why don't you sit up front?"

Sue got out and jumped in the driver's seat. The door shut and the two embraced. It was then Sue let out the cry she had been holding back the whole ride.

Harry stood before his apartment door. Visible were the markings around the picked lock. After a deep breath, with the key engaged with the lock, he turned the cylinder and slowly entered his apartment.

In front of Harry, down the hallway, a man turned the corner from the bedroom, aiming at him a pistol with an attached silencer. Wood splintered, as bullets fired in mere flashes and muffled pops hit the entrance door frame. Harry ducked into the bathroom on the left.

Harry immediately screamed in Arabic. "I got money hidden! I got money hidden!"
The gunman turned the corner, finding him sitting on the toilet, hands covering his face. The gunman pointed the gun at Harry, who looked up to find a much larger gunman standing in the door frame behind the first. Harry recognized them as the lookouts from the alley behind Bain's house.

"Where is your money?" asked the smaller gunman in Arabic.
Harry put on his best I'm scared expression. "Enough money to get both your families out of here." And again covered his face.
He put the gun closer to Harry's forehead.
"I asked you *where* is *your* money."
Harry continued the act with a shaky voice. "Behind the refrigerator. But it's rigged to explode."

On the street John and Sue sat holding hands as they listened to the news over the car radio.

Sue looked to John, who, despite what was coming over the air-waves and everything that had happened, looked as if his thoughts were elsewhere.
"What are you thinking right now?"
"Everything. Too much. You, Irish, his *kids*."
John shook his head "*Sigh*….Shit."
"I know.
"I was told a few years back that I was shooting blanks."
"You should have gotten a second opinion."
"Yeah. No Shit."

Sue looked to John and asked the question that had been suppressed and buried in the back of her head for weeks. "What is your real name?"

"Wanted petty criminal."

"You're not going to tell me?"

"Raymond. But I am going to be Jonathan Nariz even if we get out of here, whether I like it or not. Can't go back."

"What did you do?"

"In a state of depression from the wife walking out and best friend getting hit by a bus...."He took a breath. ".... in the midst of chaos, I hastily robbed a bank. Well.... I robbed work."

"Your place of work?"

"Yep." He cracked a smirk. "Without bullets. Believe it or not."

"I don't know if that's stupid or impressive. First time?"

"First and only."

"So, you're not even close to a professional thief?"

"Far from it."

"So, how did you...."

"End up here?

"Yeah."

"I took some stolen goods in a safety deposit box that was probably stored while temporarily in transit, under what I will assume was a fake account. Can't imagine why else the stuff would be in a regular bank. Anyway, these guys tracked me down. They did their homework, knew about my military background and flare for language, and gave me little choice. I took the job not even knowing what it was or where I was going."

"Tell me something about you."

"I'm Puerto Rican." He looked over with a smile. "Not even a little Arabic."

"I don't give a shit."

Again, they held each-other.

She whispered in his ear, "If I told you I was pregnant back home on the other side of the world, would you be happy?"

"There is a twisted part of me that's happy even here."

Sue noticed the city police car coming up the road behind, out of the corner of her eye. The officer appeared to be driving slowly, checking license plates.

"The cops are behind us."

John looked down to his bloody shirt, up to the cracked window, then back to the mirror in his visor.

The police stopped five cars back, questioning a taxi driver who was sleeping in his parked car.

"We don't look right," said John.

"I know."

"Put on your veil back on."

In the apartment, both guns were on Harry as he walked to the kitchen.

"Step back!" said the larger gunman.

Harry froze with hands high.

"Check the kitchen for an emergency gun."

The smaller gunman searched through the drawers, cabinets and refrigerator.

"Just look behind the refrigerator and tell me what you see."

He leaned over the counter on the left side of the refrigerator.

"I think I see a bag at the bottom."

Again, both guns pointed back to Harry.

"Ok. Get it."

Harry approached the refrigerator and grabbed the two top corners and rocked the appliance, barely moving it. Harry, stalling for time, turned with a smile and said in

244

Arabic, "So, you men knew that the conservative old guy would save his money, eh?"
Both men smirked then grinned to each other.

On the street, John and Sue sat still as the police officer questioned the man five vehicles back.

"When I say go, hit the store across the street and see what canned food is left. I'll check on Harry."
Both watched the driver behind step out of his car, quarreling with the police officer. The argument then escalated, resulting in the driver being turned, thrown and searched against his door.

"Ready?"
John and Sue quickly kissed and exchanged smiles.

"Ok. Go!"
Both slipped out of the car unnoticed.

Harry continued his show struggle with the refrigerator. After a few minutes, the gunmen grew impatient with how little Harry had moved the large appliance.

"So, how did you get it back there yourself?" asked the smaller gunman.

"I had a partner once. I think you know what happened to him on the road to the airport."
Another smirk raised by each of the men.
Harry looked to the larger gunman and gestured to the upper right corner of the refrigerator. "Pick up that corner so I can pull it."

Harry grabbed the left side of the refrigerator. The larger gunman switched the pistol to his right hand, keeping the gun away from Harry as a precaution and grabbed the right top corner with his back to the wall.

"Hey, check the door is shut," the larger gunman said to the smaller.

As Harry and the man struggled with the refrigerator, the smaller gunman walked over to the door just as John pushed it open into his face.

"I'm in bad need of a shirt, Harr…."

John, face-to-face with the gunman, immediately grabbed the armed hand.

The larger gunman turned his head, hearing the start of trouble. Harry swung open the freezer door, momentarily trapping the man against the wall with his hands up. Harry threw a left fist over the freezer door, crashing it on the man's face. Harry then reached behind to the skillet on the stove as the large gunman was straightening his right hand to shoot. Harry swung the pot, hitting the gun out of the thug's hand, over the refrigerator and down behind it.

John and the smaller gunman exchanged knees as they struggled for the weapon. Harry and the other brawled and wrestled, both exchanging dominance. John had pushed the fight to the rear of the apartment, past the kitchen and living room, into the bedroom. Harry's fight rolled into the hallway behind John's.

John pushed the man to an open window in the right corner of the room and forced the man's left hand holding the gun out the window. John removed his right hand from the man's throat and used it to shut the window, pulling his left hand out in time, but trapping the gun on the outside.

John held the window down with both hands, allowing the gunman to take full swings with his free hand at the right side of his head. John tucked his head and raised his shoulder, shielding his jaw.

The gunman grabbed the back of John's head and pushed it through the top pane of the window. John returned with a back elbow, knocking back the gunman, leaving the gun fall to an empty courtyard below. John followed up with big swings out the door to the living room, eventually knocking the man on his back.

The larger gunman, in the meantime, pushed the fight with Harry into the bathroom. Harry struggled with the rear choke as the gunman bounced him off the walls, cracking tile and plaster.

In the living room, John mounted the man's chest, continuing the beating, splitting the man's brow, punching blindly as the blood from the glass cut above his hairline filled his eyes. Lips split as John punched past, knocking out teeth. A final direct hook landing on the jaw rendered the man unconscious, allowing John to run to Harry's aid, leaving the smaller gunman a bloody mess on the floor.

In the bathroom, Harry had already lost the rear choke and was being pummeled between the bathtub and toilet.

Running in, John stomp-kicked the goon, who fell against Harry, breaking Harry's rib and temporarily wedging him between the two fixtures. John and the man started to brawl, giving Harry the chance to pull himself up.

In a pool of blood on the living room floor, the smaller gunman slowly regained consciousness and stumbled into the kitchen, opened a drawer, and pulled a knife. The man turned his head to the sounds of struggle behind the partition wall and then to the half pulled out refrigerator.

Harry struggled to get back up and jumped on the large gunman's back to reapply the rear choke. John took full swings at the man's face. Harry tried to apply pressure, but the man pulled down on Harry's arm.

In the kitchen, the smaller gunman reached down over the counter, his fingertips just inches from the money bag.

In the bathroom, John grabbed the sleeves of the large gunman's leather jacket and placed a knee in his chest as leverage to pull down the man's arms, as not to interfere with the choke.
"Put this asshole to sleep."
The man was slowly losing consciousness.
"Keep holding. Don't let go yet," pleaded Harry.
All three men fell to the floor outside the bathroom, both Harry and John strained for a moment.
"He's gone," said John.
John on the floor looked to the spot -now empty- where he left the other man. Fatigued, he stumbled up, scanning the room.
Harry remained on the floor catching his breath.
John cautiously checked each room, lastly the kitchen. With confirmation that the apartment was clear, John leaned over, his hands on his knees, to catch his breath.
"Harry, you knew these guys were here, didn't you?"
"Saw my shutter was cracked on the drive-by," he said, still laid out on the floor.
"You're a wise old fucker, aren't you, Harry."
"So, I'm told," he said as he sat up.
John looked to his right, noticing the refrigerator had been partially pulled out.

"Harry. Please tell me that the money wasn't behind the fridge."

"Shit!"

John rushed out the apartment and down to the street. Harry followed, trying to keep up while limping through each stair landing.

Both men stood in front of the building, peering down the street in each direction. They were truly a sight for all the people out front and the passersby who stared at their tattered and bloody clothes.

It was as if Harry was speaking to himself as John stared down the block. "We shouldn't be out here. We will grab some shirts and go to Irish's apartment. It's safe, he hasn't been there for weeks."

John unexpectedly ran off to Harry's car.

"Shit," said Harry, giving chase.

Harry's tires were all slashed flat. People in front of the store and on the street stood about.

John unfolded and read a note tucked under the windshield wiper. "Shit. They got Sue."

"Who?"

"I don't know. Shit!"

John crumpled the note and hastily threw it in the car. Harry looked on as John turned and looked up and down the street with his hands atop of his head, clenched, with no regard to the growing crowd of gawking pedestrians staring at two bloody foreigners in front of a vandalized vehicle. Harry went after the note and checked to see if John's duffel bag from his apartment was still in the back, but it and the money were gone with Sue.

A man holding a cell phone got out of a car and approached John, speaking broken English. "I'm trying to get a signal. The store owner is also trying to get through to the police."

       "The woman? What happened to the woman?" asked John, wide-eyed.

       "Three men...."

John interrupted, "White men?"

Harry read the note and shoved it into his pocket.

       "Yes. Three. Two took the woman and one slashed the tires."

John looked around nervously. "I'm sorry."

Harry, listening nearby, looked over, puzzled.

John, with his right hand, grabbed the car keys in the man's hand and pulled them back as he threw a kick to the groin with his right foot.

The man hunched over with an expulsion of air. John, with both hands, pushed him toward the sidewalk. The man's feet hit the curb and he fell dead weight to the concrete on his side, as his wife emerged from the store screaming.

John and Harry jumped in the man's car and drove off.

CHAPTER
THIRTY TWO

John and Harry stood before Irish's apartment door. On the door was half washed away, but still readable Arabic graffiti.

John scanned the hallway and looked back to the door. "Does that say what I think it says?"

"Spy go away or die."

"No wonder he didn't want to be here anymore."

John reached for the key as Harry pulled a tire iron from within the sleeve of a jacket he was carrying.

"Are you ready?" whispered John, with the keys in the cylinder as each stood on either side of the doorframe.

Cautiously, Harry and John stepped through the door into Irish's apartment checking room to room.

"We're good," said John. "So, what now?"

"Don't know. Can't think on an empty stomach."

Harry gathered dry goods from the kitchen cabinets.

John flopped down in a chair at the table. "I can't eat now."

"We both need to eat. We got a lot to figure out.

:

Later, after eating, Harry found himself examining the kidnappers' note. He stared down intently.

Be warned. We have the woman.
If an attempt is made at
going to the authorities or a
vain attempt of rescue, it is
at this point we will shoot her.
Nothing will happen if you stay away.

Harry grabbed a pencil and placed all the beginning letters of each line in one long oval. Inside the oval spelled vertically, was....
"BIg vaN"

Harry walked to the next room, where John had been laying on the sofa, feeling helpless and trance-like as the news played off a nearby radio. Harry stood over John, then kicked the sofa.

"What's up?"

Harry tossed the note on John's chest. "Why is anybody doing you favors?"

John sat up and looked at the note. "Fucken Louis."

"Louis?"

"The truck driver at my job. I found out when we were in the same café during Bain's sit-down. I'm sorry I didn't tell you. I didn't even tell Irish."

"No time to stay mad. This guy knows she's in danger."

"What are we going to do?"

Harry leaned over, putting a hand on John's shoulder. "I need you to get your shit together."

"She's pregnant, Harry."

"I figured as much. You still have a bloody shirt on. See what clothes are left in the drawers and take a shower."

John trudged to the bedroom. In a drawer, he reached for a towel. Underneath laid a pistol, flash-lights, two AK-47s, and boxes of ammo with extra clips. "Harry, come in here." John lifted one of the machine guns. "You're going to want to see this."

"What? Money?"

Harry walked into the bedroom, where John stood holding one of the fully automatics.

John coolly looked at Harry's surprised expression. "I guess this was the rest of Irish's note."

Harry approached the drawer to look at its contents. "Yes. Well, this changes things."

.

Later, Harry sprawled a map of Baghdad over the kitchen table and articulated his plan to rescue Sue. "A lot of these guys will be coming from this area around the industrial construction sites. This thoroughfare will be strictly military due to limited entrances, the number of lanes, and because it passes under more roads than it passes over, allowing intermittent cover. I think this is the only quick way." He pointed to a smaller, but still busy road. "We will wait here."

John looked to the map, to Harry and back to the map. "Then so be it." John shook his head. "How did it come to this?"

"We forgot that nothing comes easy to regular people. Not money. Not love."

Thinking of Jack's line at the pub a year and a half earlier, John cracked his only hint of a smile since Sue's kidnapping. "Where did you hear that?"

"Nowhere. Is it not just a evident truth?

"Yeah. Yeah, I guess it is."

CHAPTER
THIRTY THREE

John and Harry slept at Irish's apartment. All was quiet until the start of faint air-raid sirens blocks away, followed by muffled explosions in the distance. The sirens and the explosions grew louder, accompanied by anti-aircraft fire.

Harry looked to John, who was also waking.
Harry whispered, "Your country has come knocking for its sweet oil fix."
The men rolled out of bed fully clothed. Both were startled more by the knock at the door. Keeping the lights off, John sneaked over to the peep-hole. Outside stood the old lady neighbor. She kept knocking as other neighbors behind her clamored to get down the stairs.
John patiently watched until the old lady gave up and followed the others down the stairs.

Outside the door was clear.
"Hallway empty," he whispered. Turning to Harry, "So, you knew all along I was an American?"
The silhouette was enough that John didn't have to see the look on Harry's face. The cock of his head at the question painted the *Of course I fucking knew* expression.

"I know what New York, Puerto Rican Spanish sounds like."

John looked back out through the peep-hole. "Bombed by my own fucken tax dollars. Joke's on me."

John waited another minute. The lights flickered then…. darkness. With that, both men turned on their flashlights taped to their machine guns and headed off, making their way down the dark building to the street.

Turning the stairs together, John almost got knocked off balance by something Harry was carrying.

"Whoa!"

"Pay attention."

The block was pitch black. Only a couple of families jumping into their cars so far. Harry and John stood on either side of the car for a moment, taking in the surrealism of the situation.

"What's with the duffel bag?"

"The essentials," was all Harry said as he jumped in the passenger side.

John took one more look around. Through the bombs, sirens and car alarms, households could still be heard through the windows trying to keep loved ones huddled together. He jumped in and off they went.

Some streets had lights, others didn't.

The ages old *Lights Out* policy of cutting electricity to the street-lamps was being set in motion all over the city as fast as employees of the power company could carry off the security measure. Unfortunately, with cutting off the lamps, off went all the traffic signals as well. Each intersection would now grow increasingly dangerous as more citizens hit the road illegally, despite the travel ban.

There was a glow in the sky ahead. The city appeared intact until coming to the source. On the left, two residential blocks were burning rubble.

"Smart bombs, my ass," exclaimed Harry.

Ahead John saw traffic coming to a stop. "Damn it!"

"Maybe it's just some debris in the road. Don't get too close. Give yourself some room."

John stopped, leaving two car lengths in front of them. He then saw a soldier on his side, just under a hundred feet ahead, walking from vehicle to vehicle, peering into each and randomly checking identification.

"Get down!" John warned as he commenced a quick three-point k-turn on the narrow street. The soldier took notice, yelled a command to stop and got off a shot, shattering the rear window as they sped off.

"Holy shit! Why would he do that?"

Harry reached for the map without an acknowledgment or complaint and looked over his shoulder to the broken window. "They are going to do anything to maintain law and order until it all falls apart. He looked down to the map. "Make this left."

John complied, quickly cutting down a side street to bypass the check-point.

"We got to make up time," exclaimed Harry.

John slammed on the brakes when a small black pickup blew the stop sign in front of them. "I'm trying," he shot back after the near miss accident.

John continued speeding recklessly down small streets, only slowing down for intersections, where he beeped, flashed his lights and zipped through.

:

Later-

John and Harry sat parked at the engagement point that Harry sited on the map. It was an embankment along a six-lane road with a concrete barrier dividing the two sides.

Between clusters of oncoming traffic, each looked to the flashes in the sky. To the right of the car, a park was surrounded on three sides by four-story buildings.

Both men sat staring into the mirrors, silent, listening to the world explode around them.

"It's getting closer."

"Mmmm...." replied Harry.

"You coming to Cork with me?"

"Let's get through tonight first." Harry quickly regretted his curt answer, knowing John was just trying to be positive of the situation. Harry just didn't have the head to talk of a future so slim.

Each tensed with the roar of a jet that was seen in a split second in the flash of anti-aircraft fire before it banked left, engulfing all surrounding noise.

"Oh shit!" said John, gripping the wheel and hunching his shoulders.

Both men flinched as a bomb hit a building adjacent to the park.

As a former EMT John is torn as he stared at the building in flames, wondering how many of the injured he could help, but he knew it would be at the risk of missing the opportunity to save Sue. He then questioned whether that opportunity would ever arrive. The choice of staying stationary, leaving someone to die so another might live, wrenched his stomach. He can't believe he put himself in this position -*back in Baghdad twelve years later.*

As an ex-military man, Harry would have jumped all over John for not keeping his eyes on the road as traffic started to build, but he knew his friend's

258

concentration has been compromised by worrying for Sue.

Harry, vigilantly watching the road, sat up when noticing the lights of a large van standing out from all the smaller cars coming up the road behind. "I think this is it."

A white Mercedes sprinter van passed, followed by two smaller, white Toyota minivans, two hundred feet behind it, running close together. All three vehicles were in the middle lane, staying with the flow of traffic as not to attract attention. John waited for the last Toyota to pass, along with a few other cars, before merging into traffic with the lights off.

In the front of the sprinter van sat a young crew member no older than twenty-three, next to him, the Captain. Behind the passenger seat, Sue sat leaning against the side wall with one hand cuffed to a flat railing for cargo strapping that bordered the entire back of the van. To Sue's left, sat Louis. Across from Louis, behind the driver, was Remy. In the back, sat the Lieutenant and three other men, guns and equipment in hand.

In the Toyotas sat six men each, a mix of young Caucasian French and black men from the sub-Saharan country of Chad.

Chad had emerged from the French colonial rule that stretched from the west coast to the center of the continent until its steady unraveling after the Second World War. A poor, undeveloped country encumbered by civil war and military coups, it was a perfect place to find Arabic-speaking mercenaries.

Traffic was congested in pockets, but moving steadily. John struggled to get into a surprise position when he noticed the irregularly large and high head-lamps in the rear-view mirror. "What do you think?"

Harry looked over his shoulder. "This will work. Get behind this thing and we can engage from their left."

As the road opened up, all cars, including John and Harry's, moved to the right, letting a large, wide military crane pass.

John and Harry cut back to the middle lane tailgating the crane, which moved a little faster than the flow of traffic.

In the second Toyota van, the driver radioed the other two vans of the approaching crane. All three vans moved to the right lane.

John maneuvered from the tailgating position to the left lane, using the crane as a barrier as it slowly started to pass the two Toyota vans.

In the second van, one of the driver-side passengers watched the wheels of Harry's car through the undercarriage of the crane as it passed, unaware of the coming ambush.

Harry also looked through the underside of the crane to the wheels of the vans. Harry turned in his seat, positioning himself to shoot as the crane was about to get within five feet from rear bumper of the first Toyota. "Get ready. Ready....Now!"

John hit the Gas, bringing the first Toyota van into the line of fire for Harry.

For the first Toyota, Harry's car came out from their left, shining the flashlight taped to his gun in their eyes.

Harry sprayed the van with bullets, appearing to hit most -if not all- inside, as men slouched forward or back. The van quickly veered off the side of the road.

The second Toyota hit the brakes, taking the van out of the line of fire.

Inside the cab of the crane, two soldiers looked to each other with confusion. "What's going on?"

"Stay in this lane. Bait them around," commanded Harry.

In the sprinter van, the driver looked to the rear-view mirror, but the backup vans were nowhere in sight. He called on the radio with no response.

Harry positioned to shoot out the rear window.

The Toyota jumped in the left lane. Out of the rear windows on both sides, men were already postured, shooting, causing Harry to take cover before he got off a shot.

John sped up and cut in front of the crane. "Shit! That was a bad Idea."
"More aggressive than I expected." Harry looked through the broken back window, seeing a light come on in the cab of the crane. "Quick, get to the right lane."

Inside the cab of the crane, the soldier sitting passenger side grabbed his AK-47. "Who are these guys?" He reached behind him into a camouflage duffel bag for magazines. The driver sped up.

The remaining Toyota van slowly crept up the left side of the crane.

John then jumped to the right lane, slowing up just enough to let half the crane pass.

The Toyota now cut in front of the crane and hit the brakes intermediately, so the gunman at the right rear window could get a clear shot.

John slowed each time to avoid taking a hit.

The driver of the sprinter van witnessed the flashes of the muzzles in the mirror. "We got trouble."

The Captain also saw. He sneered at Sue as he walked to the back. Remy looked to Sue, who closed her eyes and gently rubbed her abdomen with her free hand.

"That's it!" declared the soldier in the crane as he slid open his side of the windshield. He fired down on the roof of the Toyota. It was killing fish in a barrel.

The van of dead men, momentarily pushed by the crane, veered to the left, skidded sideways, and was crushed between the four-foot divider and the left side of the crane.

The driver of the sprinter witnessed the second Toyota's demise. "Shit," he said, as he stomped the pedal, accelerating.

The soldier loaded another clip and leaned out the right-side window, shooting at John and Harry.

John jammed on the brakes and swung to the middle lane behind the crane. The crane slowed to make a wide right turn at an intersection. Immediately, John floored the pedal, trying to catch up with the sprinter van.

Both drivers sped through traffic, cutting off other drivers, bumping cars and narrowly avoiding serious collision.

"You ready?" asked the Captain, who, along with another, braced both sides of the van with one hand and gripping a lanyard worn by the smallest of the mercenaries.

"Yes."

The back door of the van quickly swung open. The young man leaned out, firing at Harry and John, who distanced themselves, yet Harry still maintained returning fire, aiming low, looking to take out the tires.

"Close the door. Save the ammo."

A police car now chased John and Harry.

"Are you seeing this shit?" asked John, looking into the rearview mirror.

"It was only a matter of time," said Harry as he took stock of what was left of ammo between them. "Going to need yours too," he said, reaching for John's gun.

The chase had headed toward a traffic circle, where there sat a checkpoint with a number of military vehicles.

"What are they going to do?" asked John.

"It doesn't matter. We can't stop either."

In the sprinter van, the driver noticed the police car in chase as they approached the traffic circle. "Captain?"

"Go through it."

The driver bumped the car in front, jumped the curb, and blew through the checkpoint. John and Harry followed, the police following them and now three military jeeps with mounted machine guns left the checkpoint to join the pursuit.

The Captain walked back to the passenger seat, stopped, and glared at Louis, clenching his jaw. Louis looked back nervously. The Captain pulled his pistol and fired as the driver swerved to avoid a burning car on the road. Sue ducked and screamed as the first bullet hit Louis in the shoulder, the second and third piercing through the wall behind her.

Louis lunged for the gun and grappled with the Captain. The Lieutenant grabbing Louis, and Remy grabbing the Captain, finally separated the two men.
Remy pulled his pistol and put it to the Captain's temple from behind. "Hand it over!"

"What the hell is going on?" the driver asked nervously.

"Just keep driving!" the Lieutenant said with urgency.
The Captain relinquished the weapon to Remy.
Remy kept his gun on the Captain and pointed the Captain's gun at the Lieutenant. "Stay right there."

The Lieutenant, freezing, backed off and sat down with Louis and the other three men in back.

"Sit down, Captain."
The Captain sat next to Sue, and Remy sat across from them. In the van, all eyes were on Remy.

Harry and John kept up the chase through the obstacle course of chaos that the Baghdad streets had become.

"He's a traitor! He sold us…."

"Shut up! You've said enough. You've done enough. Over a year in this shitty country. The lies, the murder, and now the kidnapping and endangering of a pregnant woman."

All the men glanced to Sue.

The Captain swallowed a lump in his throat. "You're finished."

"I don't give a shit." Remy looked to Sue. "Doctor. Please tell everybody why I don't give a shit."

Sue looked to Remy, but said nothing.

"Go ahead. Tell them what you told me in your clinic months ago, after you had me go for tests at the city hospital."

"You are well into stage-four lymphoma."

"Tell them the rest of it."

"It is most likely as a result of the undiagnosed and untreated HIV infection, possibly acquired through intravenous drug use," said Sue, quietly, yet clear enough for all to hear. She said it with the same sympathetic tone she'd used when she had uttered it in her office the first time.

"I told them how to find us. I wrote the note." Purposely looking to all the men in back, Remy continued, "I'm your traitor." Looking to Louis, he said, "Sorry I wasn't a more amiable partner."

Louis just nodded in return.

He then locked eyes with Sue, who again had her hand on her abdomen. "And to you, Doctor…." He paused. "Congratulations. Good people like you *should* have children. As for me, I'm not going to face my children in France, a dying shell of a man who profited off such a sin as this has been."

Louis and the three young men were still as the Lieutenant inched closer to Remy.

Remy locked out his arm pointing the pistol at the Lieutenant. "That's far enough."

"How long are you going to keep us all at bay, Remy?"

"I don't plan to anymore."

Remy pointed the gun from the Lieutenant to under his own chin. The Lieutenant lunged forward as Remy pulled both triggers, shooting himself in the head and the Captain in the heart. Sue screamed, and all flinched, including the driver, who tucked his head to the steering wheel.

The Captain, eyes wide, slumped farther down on the bench, in a leaning back position. The Lieutenant and the men in back stared with a sense of apathy, for it been too long in Iraq for everyone and now the big payoff was all unraveling.

Louis looked to his partner, feeling sorry it was the first time in years with respect. But the moment of reflection was brief and no one had to say anything for all to quickly get back to the situation at hand.

John closed the distance despite the diesel eight-cylinder in the Mercedes. It was only the bad handling of the bulky van around obstacles in the given situation that has allowed John to catch up in the beat-up fifteen-year-old four-cylinder Saab. Harry leaned out the window to position for another shot at the wheels.

The van's back door cracked open.

Harry slipped back into the car, fearing heavy machine-gun fire. "Pull back again! Pull back!"

Out of the van tumbled two bodies. It's a blur as Remy and the Captain's bodies violently rolled against the pavement.

"Oh my God!" yelled John, his voice cracking.

"It's not Sue! It's not Sue," said Harry as the bodies passed close to him on the passenger side. "Keep driving. Keep driving."

"What the fuck is going on?"

"Mutiny."

The chase continued with narrowly missed accidents for all six vehicles, involving other motorists, burnt abandoned cars and debris in the road.

The sprinter van broke through an orange-and-white road barricade now, putting all six vehicles on the approach to a two-span destroyed bridge over the Tigris River.

"Ok. Try it again." The Lieutenant along with another crew member held the lightweight man from falling out as he shot from the back door. Harry returned fire, finishing the last of the clip.

A bullet hit Harry's left front tire. The blowout caused the car to veer to the left, just before the divide in the road, separating the approach to the north and south spans of the blown-up bridge.

"Shit! What now. What now?"

Harry didn't have a solution, only an answer, "Ok, just keep going."

Unable to turn back, John and Harry followed the van parallel from the north span. The tire had frayed and turned to a rim of sparks as the police were catching up.

"How much ammo is left?" asked John.

"Maybe half a clip and what's in the pistol."

On the south bridge span, the van stopped about fifty feet from the edge of the bridge. The military jeeps stopped further back another two hundred feet. In between them were bodies and abandoned and burned vehicles.

On the north span, the police following John and Harry stopped at the first piece of large debris on the road, allowing the creation of strategic distance.

The police knew the Saab had nowhere to go, yet didn't know how desperate or how much firepower Harry and John had at their disposal, considering the firefight with the larger vehicle and the brazen running through of a military checkpoint.

John, knowing the police have stayed back for now, cautiously wove the Saab through the wreckage as he kept an eye on the other span. He stopped short of the last military jeep on the south span, whose soldier at the mounted belt-fed 7.62mm already had John and Harry in his sights.

A ranking officer in the middle jeep looked between the Saab and the Sprinter van. "Don't shoot yet. If they are CIA or MI6, I want them for questioning," he said, speaking into his radio to the other two military vehicles. He then said into his cell phone, "I need immediate contact with the commander at Southern River District Police!"

On the south span, the Iraqi military jeeps remained in position for the possible fire-fight.

Inside the sprinter van, the crew looked to one another. From outside came a command to surrender, first in Arabic, then moments after, in English.

"Keep your eyes on the mirrors," said the lieutenant to the driver.

Harry, without taking his eyes from the soldier pointing the 308-caliber asked, "What exactly do you plan on doing?"

"What would you do, Harry?"

"Twenty-plus years in the military and never confronted with this. I suppose wait. The bombs are still dropping. They should realize that there are more important places to be. But when would it be?"

"I'm going to tell them."

"What?"

John threw his hands out the window above the roof of the car and postured his feet to climb out with his hands in full view.

Harry grabbed at his shirt. "No. Don't do that!"

John grabbed the radio antenna on the car frame and pulled one leg out at a time. With hands raised, he walked closer to the four-foot concrete wall and water that separated the bridge spans, shouting in Arabic repetitively, "There is a kidnapped pregnant woman in the van! There is a kidnapped pregnant woman in the van!"

Sue closed her tear-filled eyes and smiled as everyone in the Sprinter van and the soldiers outside listened intensely.

Louis looked over, "A good man, Johnny."

"I knew that already, Louis."

Louis, already guilt-ridden, looked back to his shoes.

In the scope of a rifle, John's head fell into the crosshairs.

On the north span, Harry slipped into the driver's seat and watched John carefully from the car, until a bomb exploding nearby, coinciding with a gunshot, had him duck low in the seat. John dropped to the pavement.

All tensed in the Sprinter van. The Lieutenant leaned over the driver to get a look in the side mirror.

Harry looked in the rear-view mirror to the Police Special Tactics Unit van beside the original police car, then to John laying on the pavement, by the wall, but very much alive.

John yelled out Sue's name as he laid on his back, holding the nick of the bullet to the back of his head.
Harry returned fire over his shoulder, finishing the last of the AK-47 rounds through the rear window, then blindly sped towards John as he crouched as low as possible, allowing the concrete barrier on the side to provide cover as the military jeeps now targeted the runaway vehicle.
Harry reached across, opening the passenger door. "Hurry, get in!"
"What about Sue?"
"They're not shooting at her. They're shooting at us! Get in!"

Shots from the mounted machine guns on the opposite bridge span sent concrete debris through the air as John crawled to the car, where it was blocked from shots of accuracy by the police due to abandoned vehicles.

The 308-caliber rounds from the military blasted out the windshield and cut through the front door frames of the Saab on either side, to the point the roof sank down in front. Both, John and Harry bled from shattering debris.

"There's no turning back. You know how to swim?" asked Harry.

"Yeah. Shit!"

Harry floored the gas. "I don't know if we have a clear landing."

"Fuck it! Go!"

"Ok get ready."

All were taken aback by what looked like suicide at the expense to avoid capture. More gaping holes were delivered to its roof and upper frame as the Saab raced from the illumination of police lights and building fires on the bank of the river and into the darkness at the edge.

At the end of the bridge, Harry and John first bore the impact of clipping a burnt abandoned vehicle and then another as they had surprisingly landed on to the missing span of road, which was barely attached on the other side.

The police took a little time before turning around to join the standoff on the other side.

The impact cut the engine. Harry tried to restart with no avail. Worse yet, the hard landing had disengaged the transmission, and the steep incline had the car sliding to the river below.

"Hold on!" yelled John, as the car slid down the broken roadway into the river.

"Grab the duffel bag! Grab it!"

South span-

"No choice, but to shoot our way out," asserted the Lieutenant.

The driver looked to the empty south span. "Let's do what they did."

"They're dead," he replied, dismissing the young man's suggestion. "Get ready."
The crew prepared to jump out and fight.

"Uncuff the woman and let her go," he ordered the men. "You can go now," he said dismissively, while checking ammunition.
Sue rubbed her wrists. "Where am I going? To jail? I'm not going anywhere."
The Lieutenant gave Sue a long look up and down. He then turned to Louis and his injury. "Sit in the front seat with her. Keep your head down."
The driver climbed in the back, giving Louis the front seat. Sue sat passenger side. Louis looked to the young driver and gave him a subtle shake of his head. The young man caught in the bravado of orders, saw the message, but did not acknowledge it.

The Lieutenant opened the door, shooting and jumping out, followed by the other four men. The young driver, being last, was immediately shot against the door.

Louis and Sue crouched down in the seats, hiding from the soldiers. Bullets whizzed past, hitting the windshield as the back doors to the van swung wide open

Outside, one by one of the French crew was cut down by the superior firepower of the Iraqi military, who inched up from one abandoned vehicle to the next. The truck's mounted machine gun shot through cars and trucks, where some of the mercenaries hunkered unsuccessfully for cover.

Louis looked to Sue as she cried. She sank lower in the seat, cradling both hands around her abdomen as two bullets passed through the seat above her head.

Louis started kicking out the windshield. Sue followed suit.

A bullet hit Louis in the right hand, but he continued kicking. He pushed the glass out of the windshield frame and to the pavement. They jumped out, running, with bullets flying overhead, and leaped off the edge of the bridge as the last of the French crew members were shot dead.

The Iraqi soldiers advanced on the van. They saw nobody and radioed back to the jeeps. One soldier looked to the kicked-out windshield in front of the van and walked to the edge of the bridge. Frustrated and confused, he shook his head. Aside from the flashes in the sky, Baghdad was dark, and he couldn't see much besides a building fire on the other side of the river. *What just happened? Who were these people?* A ranking officer called him back.

Below, Louis and Sue sat against a bridge pillar. Louis draped his arm and jacket around Sue.

"Psst...." came a whisper from the black.
Sue and Louis turned to see John and Harry float up on a piece of debris. The duffel bag in the water, its strap over Harry's shoulder, but now buoyant.
"Come aboard," whispered Harry.
Sue jumped in the water, followed by Louis. Sue and John embraced and kissed. Louis grabbed the float with his good hand, exchanging a nod and a crack of a smile with Harry and John.
Sue asked John, "What now?"
"The water is not freezing but still cold. Keep our heads down and float on and off in the direction of the coalition forces," John replied with a sense of defeat. Although John was grateful for Sue's safety, having to go to the source of all this destruction for

273

help didn't feel right, as he thought about all the people he had met throughout the year and wondering,…. what of their fate. *Coworkers? The friendly shopkeepers? Where is Asera and the baby I saved? Or for that matter all the young children from the clinic?* No doubt everyone felt the same. But for Sue there was more.

"John, I'm pregnant. I just can't float for miles. I'm going to need to eat and drink.

Harry pulled out a bottle of water and a ready-to-eat food ration packet from the bag. "I thought of that, Mom. We are all going to be ok."

John smiled. "Wise old fucker, Harry."

"This time I will not be modest and agree."

The four floated south on the Tigris, silence between them as they watched Baghdad burn.

Louis was the first to speak, after what seemed like miles. "I don't feel it now, but one day I'll smile, knowing those bastards in Europe never got those plates."

John looked over to him. "I'm beginning to think no one was supposed to."

"Oh, someone got them. Just not you," said Sue, snarkily.

Harry looked over to Sue with a concurring nod and grin. "You can bet someone did."

Epilogue

A young man of fourteen finished positioning a frame on the wall, stepped back and turned to his twelve-year-old sister. "So, what do you think?"

"What are they supposed to be?"

"I don't know, but they look cool."

The father stepped into the room, a burly man in his early forties. "Hey, we have to go for a ride to…." He froze upon noticing the addition to his son's bedroom. "Where did you get that?" he asked with changing expression.

The young girl sneaked out of the room.

"You better not have gotten that from the museum," he said, pointing, making the boy flinch.

"No."

"Where did you get that?" he asked, getting in his son's face and pointing at the frame.

"From Saddam's palace. I swear!"

He cuffed his son in the head and yelled, "Our country is in ruins, and you're out stealing?"

"I wasn't stealing."

The mother, who heard the last exchange from the hallway, entered the room and gasped at the sight of the object.

"Get in the car. We're going to your aunt's to help fix the roof," he yelled, pointing out the door.

The boy winced as he passed his dad and out of the room.

Out the door he yelled, "We will talk about this later."

The parents remained in the room. The man walked up to the frame of plates and stared.

"You don't think he was at the museum, do you?"

"Said he got it from Saddam's palace," he answered, with a calmer tone.

The mother shook her head. "Are you going to let him keep it?"

"I suppose. Even though I'm the one who fought for this country." He raised two fingers along with his voice. "Twice!"

The man continued to stare at the frame.

"Do you really want it?" asked the mother with a smirk.

He looked over his shoulder to his wife behind with an expression of annoyance, but not all the way around, he instead turned back to the frame. "No."

The parents sat fixated for a moment.

"Do you think it's valuable?"

The man leaned in even closer. "Nah...."

Afterword

In the days following the bombing, American news broadcasts repeatedly showed scenes of looting throughout Iraqi urban centers, Baghdad being the worst, due to its size and higher military targeting.

In a press conference, Secretary of Defense Donald Rumsfeld downplayed the extent of the looting of private, state and cultural institutions, saying-

"It's the same man with the same vase shown on the news over and over again."

While true, that for sensational effect with ratings in mind, the most dramatic and clearest footage was used of a young man in his mid-twenties running with a three-foot vase through a street of rubble, was the most circulated and looped throughout all major networks supplied by the Associated Press.

Limited stories were aired exposing the gravity of bombing a region primarily comprised of desert and cities dependent upon infrastructure to disseminate goods and services for the basic necessities of food, water and disposal of refuse.

While *STEALING HISTORY* is a fictional back-story of the very real, professionally orchestrated and obviously avarice driven theft of the Iraq National Museum of Art during the bombing of Baghdad, we will never know whether it was profit or panic that exacerbated the situation when copper motor windings were scrapped from domestic water plant distribution pumps and from waste treatment plant grinders, leaving many at the mercy of water delivery trucks and exposed to the health hazards of raw sewage running open in the streets in many of the largest cities.

In the end, the sad reality, historically repeated yet not often discussed, is that in the chaotic environment of natural disaster or war, looting, if not motivated by the monetary gain it may serve, -or does serve- is an unfortunate means to an end to initiate barter for the citizen who does not expect that societal order will be restored before possible dehydration or starvation.

www.ingramcontent.com/pod-product-compliance
Lightning Source LLC
Chambersburg PA
CBHW061553170626
46811CB00001B/191